Cross + Catherine
THE COMPANION

BETHANY-KRIS

Copyright © 2018 by Bethany-Kris. All Rights Reserved.

WARNING: The unauthorized distribution or reproduction of this copyrighted work is illegal. No parts of this work may be used, reproduced, or printed without expressed written consent by the author/publisher. Exceptions are made for small excerpts used in reviews.

Published by Bethany-Kris

www.bethanykris.com

eISBN 13: 978-1-988197-57-9

Print ISBN 13: 978-1-988197-58-6

Cover Art © Bethany-Kris

Editor: Elizabeth Peters

This is work of fiction. Characters, names, places, corporations, organizations, institutions, locales, and so forth are all the product of the author's imagination, or if real, used fictitiously. Any resemblance to a person, living or dead, is entirely coincidental.

For all the lovers of this series and couple. I hope it's everything you wanted, and beyond.

Contents

ONE	7
ALWAYS ERA SHORTS	12
TWO	13
THREE	19
FOUR	22
FIVE	28
SIX	36
SEVEN	40
EIGHT	48
NINE	53
REVERE ERA SHORTS	58
TEN	59
ELEVEN	64
TWELVE	70
THIRTEEN	75
FOURTEEN	79
FIFTEEN	83
SIXTEEN	87
SEVENTEEN	93
UNRULY ERA SHORTS	99
EIGHTEEN	100
NINETEEN	105
TWENTY	109
TWENTY-ONE	115
TWENTY-TWO	122
TWENTY-THREE	128
TWENTY-FOUR	133
TWENTY-FIVE	141
TWENTY-SIX	147

TWENTY-SEVEN	151
TWENTY-EIGHT	157
TWENTY-NINE	164
THIRTY	170
THIRTY-ONE	177

The Beginning

    Catherine Cecelia Marcello Donati (yes, she kept her maiden name before her married name) is an enigma. Surrounded by beautiful things, with her neck draped in a diamond necklace, that likely costs more than my small car, she sips on cheap wine and admits she's got a taste for the European band her nineteen-year-old son—Nazio—enjoys when I ask about her musical tastes.

    "But don't tell him that," she tells me, "because apparently, that's not cool, and I don't want to listen to him go on about it."

    "What about Cece?" I ask. "Or is she out of that stage in her life, now?"

    Catherine rolls her eyes. "Cece was my little twin from the moment she learned how to talk. Nothing I do could be uncool when she idolized me."

    Despite the way she says it so offhandedly, almost dismissively, I can hear warmth in her words, too. A love so strong, it's tangible, really.

    There's respect there, too.

    When I point it out, Catherine simply says, "Cece's earned her respect."

    Nothing more.

Nothing less.

So is the way of their life. While she's open about discussing her family and husband, any remarks she gives me about business is short, and to the point.

They just don't talk about business.

Her daughter's raising was a bit unconventional, too, by all standards. The daughter of a Queen Pin, Cece, saw and did more things than most grown women before she was even a teenager. She grew up watching her mother run a criminal empire, and the same with her father, too.

Although, always more her mother.

I'm curious, and so I ask, "Do you think you should have given Cece a ... normal life? Maybe kept her out of harm's way more than you did when you always had her following along when you did business?"

Catherine thinks about it for a long while, but doesn't immediately answer. No, she nurses her wine instead, and mulls it over.

Finally, she settles on a simple, "No."

I press, but it remains the same.

No.

"Why not?"

"Because she is my child, and not anyone else's," Catherine says. "She grew up in our life, not someone else's. Rose-tinted glasses are dangerous eyewear."

And of course, she's right.

"And also, not very cute," she adds, smirking.

A joke, it seems.

Yeah, she's an enigma.

We're sitting in her library surrounded by the smell of leather, and old books. This is her happy place—where she comes to relax. "Cross has his music room," she says with a smirk, "and I have this." She doesn't mind, though, because books are an escape, and, "Every woman occasionally needs an escape."

"Even when your husband is Cross Donati?" I dare to ask.

Catherine tips her head to the side a bit, and nods. "Sometimes, more so because my husband is Cross Donati."

He can be fickle, she admits. He's easy to please, and then tough to understand all at the same time. Together, it's always just them, but sometimes, she knows he needs space, too. Like she does.

They're them.

They're together.

They are an *us*.

But they are also a woman and a man. A woman who needs to be alone sometimes, and a man who needs one room to himself in his house that has nothing to do with his brilliant, genius son, and his very diva-like daughter.

Although, now their kids are nineteen and twenty-three. They don't live at home anymore, but Catherine assures it doesn't matter. They still need their spaces. They still respect what the other wants, and they talk more than they fight.

Catherine gets it.

I think I might get it, too.

"But we fight, too," she adds, grinning a little.

They argue about things all married couples argue about. She steals his blankets, and he leaves his shit all over the house. She puts too much sugar in his coffee, and he can't wait until a single thing is cooked before he has to, as she says, "Stick a fucking spoon in it. Drives me *nuts*."

I laugh.

So does she.

So yeah, they need their space sometimes.

Like all normal, married couples.

"Here is where I release everything weighing me down," she says before sipping from her glass of cheap red wine. "And that comes on so strong sometimes, that it surprises me. After all these years, and it's still there, you know?"

Depression, she means.

Her struggle with mental illness is one I know all too well, and one she has been open about for a good portion of her life. She doesn't treat it like a plague anymore, and she knows it's never really going to go away.

"Kind of seasonal," she adds, pointing to the window where it's bright and clear outside. A summer day, actually. "When the weather is good, I feel good."

But when it's cold and damp and dark, she feels it creeping in. But she almost always knows when it's coming now, and she can better handle it.

"Going to Cali helps," she says.

"Good weather," I agree.

When I ask if she has anything to tell those who struggle like she does, Catherine doesn't even think about the question. Maybe it's the fact she's been battling this for years, and her mantra is always close by.

Nonetheless, her advice is on point.

As always.

"You have to be open," she explains, "otherwise, how does anyone around you know how to help when you need it the most?"

Because sometimes, silent screams are all you can do.

And no one can hear those right away.

Catherine picks up her phone when it dings, and glances at the screen with a smile. "Cece," she says when I raise a brow in question.

All too soon, we'll be walking down Fifth Avenue because her daughter has finally come back from her honeymoon, and she wants me to join her and Cece on a shopping spree.

"We don't do that very often," Catherine adds, "but I'm giving her a little break before she needs to get back to work."

"And how do you feel about that—Cece being in the family business, I mean?"

I wonder if she'll answer, since business is supposed to be off the table.

She surprises me.

She tells me this felt normal. That watching Cece grow from a young girl to a young woman was normal, too. And, she adds, "It always kind of felt like this was where Cece was going to end up, but we didn't know how long it would take for her to settle on it."

Catherine raises a perfectly manicured eyebrow. It kind of strikes me how much she looks like the red-headed woman in the picture next to the leather chair she rests in. Her mother, Catrina. The dark hair and green eyes come from her father, but she's definitely her mother's child.

"Being a Queen Pin and a mother must be ..."

"It's a challenge, but I like those."

She offers it like there's nothing else to ask or say, and so I don't ask anything more in that vein.

My gaze drifts to the photo on the stand again of her mother. Catherine catches me watching it, and smiles.

"Do you know there are some who consider your mother to be a very cold woman?" I ask.

Catherine's laughter is both light, and bitter. Sharp like glass, and yet sweet like maple syrup. I think if that person was close enough to feel the coldness radiating from Catherine at the idea of someone disliking her mother, they would turn into ice.

Her mother was the best mother, she explains, her tone warming again. The kind of mother that supported her children no matter what, and always took their interests into perspective before inserting her own.

"And she loves us," Catherine adds, shrugging, "she has always loved us even in times when we didn't give her very much to love. I would like to know what is so cold about that."

I couldn't tell her.

I don't know, either.

And with that question, it's clear Catherine is done for the moment. All it takes is the suggestion that someone might criticize her mother, and she shuts down.

It's clear—*obvious*.

Her mother is like her.

They are similar.

They are equally strong women with lives that shaped them into who they are today. A person might not like their choices, or their way of living, or even how they chose to do things, but it is not your life.

It is theirs.

Queens.

This is the queen's home, and so she should not be insulted.

Still, I dare one more question. "What do you hope the fans of your stories will find within this companion?"

Catherine stills.

Quiets.

Smiles.

"I hope they find our life is good," she murmurs, "and that alone makes them happy."

I, too, hope it makes you happy.

—Bethany-Kris

Always Era Shorts

The Market

Catherine POV

    Catherine's gaze shifted between her father's Mercedes waiting to leave from the drop-off line, and Cross sitting on his friend's car. Dante would expect his daughter to go right into the school's entrance considering the bell was about to signal the start of classes. She had other plans for the day that didn't include sitting in classroom after classroom.
    Plans her dad definitely wouldn't like.
    Finally, her father's Mercedes got an opening to leave the growing line up of cars. Soon, her father was out of sight entirely. Catherine checked across the lot to see where her older brother, Michel, had gone to. She caught sight of Michel's back just as he headed through the entrance doors of the upper Academy.
    All safe, she thought.
    Michel probably wouldn't have ratted her out, though. He was good like that—she just wasn't interested in hearing one of his lectures. Like he was a freaking angel or something that never did anything wrong.
    Catherine ignored the call of one of her friends, and her cousin, as she headed across the parking lot. At the sight of her coming his way, Cross pushed off the hood of Zeke's car, and landed to his feet with wide smile.

He was already reaching for her outstretched hand to take by the time she got to him.

She still wasn't sure what they were. Boyfriend and girlfriend. Dating or not. Just friends. Something. Nothing.

It had only been a month since that day at the beach when she kissed him, so for now, Catherine figured it didn't really matter. She liked Cross, and hanging out with him. He kept the idiots away from her, and made the transition into the new school easier. She didn't care what he and she were at the moment.

They could get that all sorted later.

Right?

"Ready to have some fun?" Cross asked.

"Still didn't say what we were doing."

Zeke's head popped out of the driver's window. "How does a movie and food in Hell's Kitchen sound?"

Catherine looked to Cross. "The city?"

He shrugged. "We'll be back in lots of time. Don't worry about that. No one will even know you skipped out on classes."

Oh, she didn't doubt that for a minute. It was just that Catherine was not supposed to go into the city without an enforcer to watch her. Not to mention, she had never even gone to the city without being accompanied by someone in her family.

Cross must have seen the hesitance warring in Catherine's eyes. "We don't have to go, Catherine."

Don't be stupid. People skip school all the damn time. It's the city. What's going to happen to you in a freaking city?

"We're going," she told him.

Cross took her bag with a laugh, and tossed it into the back of Zeke's car. Cross climbed into the front while Catherine slid into the backseat alone. They had just pulled out of the school's parking lot when the bell finally rang behind them.

"Are we going to pick up—what's her name … Amanda?" Catherine asked.

Zeke grunted something Catherine couldn't understand, and then grumbled more under his breath. The sound alone made her cock an eyebrow. Apparently, something had happened there, and she missed out on it.

"They're broken up again," Cross said when Catherine looked to him for an explanation. "No Amanda today, but maybe next time."

"Not gonna be a fucking next time, either," Zeke said sharply. "I am done with her shit. Drives me crazy."

Cross nodded, and scoffed. "Right, man. Like you two don't do this shit every other week, then? We're playing games now, I guess."

Catherine managed to hide her giggle by slapping a palm over her mouth. Cross always did that kind of stuff to people—*all* people. Teachers, friends, and whoever else stepped into his path. He liked to call them out when they gave him the chance. She thought people might learn their lesson after the first couple of times.

Zeke was proof they did not learn.

"You know what," Zeke said to Cross, "how about you just shut up."

Cross flipped Zeke the middle finger, but didn't say a word otherwise.

Zeke glanced in the rearview mirror at Catherine. "Do you have any place that you want to visit in the Kitchen since that's where we're heading?"

"Me?"

"I'm looking at you, aren't I?"

"Be nice," Cross warned.

He added a punch to Zeke's shoulder to make his point. Zeke barely reacted at all to the hit.

"Yeah, you," Zeke said, still looking at Catherine. "Anywhere you want to go, or what?"

Catherine had to think about it. She had only been to Hell's Kitchen a couple of times before. Usually, her time in the city—when she went—was spent in upper Manhattan, on Fifth Avenue, or inside one of her family's upscale restaurants. She had gotten to spend the day in Hell's Kitchen once with her aunt, Kim. One place stood out the most in her memory.

"Could we go to The Annex?"

Cross looked back at her. "Seriously?"

"Yeah, the market, you know. Why are you looking at me like that?"

"Maybe because he might think it's a little low-key for your tastes," Zeke suggested.

Catherine frowned. "What's that supposed to mean? Like I'm too spoiled or something?"

"Yeah—"

Cross punched Zeke again. A lot harder the second time, and it shut his friend up instantly.

Zeke glared. "Do that again, Cross."

Cross ignored his friend, and turned back to Catherine. "Yeah, we can go to The Annex."

She settled into the backseat. "Okay."

"Where's he going?" Catherine asked when Zeke left the table.

The older teenager headed out of the diner without a look back. His phone had chimed with a call or something, but he hadn't even checked it before leaving the table.

"Amanda," Cross said before taking a bite of pizza.

"He didn't even look at his phone. How do you know that?"

"The ringtone—he uses that one for her calls."

"Oh."

"You gonna eat, or …?"

Catherine laughed, and reached for the fork next to her plate. Just the strange look on Cross's face was enough to make her hesitate.

"What?" she asked.

"You're not seriously going to use that, are you?"

"The fork?"

"Yeah," he said.

Catherine was so confused that it wasn't even funny. Yet, there Cross sat looking at her like she was some kind of strange creature, and serious as could be.

"Well, I was going to use it," she said, "but not if you keep staring at me like that."

He continued chewing on his bite of pizza, and looking at her all the while. Catherine looked away, and then back at him. *Still staring.*

"Stop it, Cross."

With a laugh, he set his pizza down, and wiped his mouth with a napkin. "Sorry. It's just … nobody eats pizza with a fork, Catherine."

"Liar. Lots of people do."

"Name two."

"Me," she said. "My mom."

"Name two more."

"My brother and dad."

Cross's brow furrowed. "Really?"

Catherine shrugged. "Ma's weird about people making a mess."

"Huh."

"Yep."

Cross nodded at her plate. "Well, your mom isn't here now, so no forks."

"Don't tell me how to eat my food, Cross."

"Jesus, Catherine, why don't you just pick up that slice of pizza and enjoy it with your hands and mouth like God intended for it to be enjoyed?"

"What, like you don't think I can or something?"

He shrugged, but said nothing.

Catherine took that as a challenge. She picked up the slice of pizza on her plate, and bit into it with a sly smile. Grease and cheese spread over her fingertips, and made a damn mess of her hands. She did her best to ignore it, though.

All the while, Cross's smirk grew to almost smug proportions. Catherine finished her bite, set the rest of the slice down on the plate, and grabbed a napkin. A napkin Cross already had waiting for her, and handed over with a laugh. She cleaned all the grease from her fingers and mouth that she could before he gave her a second napkin.

"I know what you did—tricking me into eating with my hands, I mean."

Cross winked. "Had to mess with you. Use the fork, Catherine. My mom does, too."

Catherine rolled her eyes, and grabbed the fork. "Jerk."

"Am not."

"Kind of," she replied, doing her best to ignore his gaze.

Catherine heard Cross's pizza hit the plate. Then, he caught her wrist, and tugged gently. She just turned in the seat to face him, and he kissed her.

Soft and sweet, and never more than she was willing to give. He always left the option of more up to her. It was both thrilling and new, yet familiar and comforting at the same time. A mixture of too many things that made her heart clench, and her stomach do flips.

All too soon, Cross was pulling away. Catherine had the strongest urge to pull him back in for another kiss almost instantly. She didn't, but that was only because Zeke was finally making his way back to the table.

Zeke dropped into the chair with a grin. "Ready to go?"

Catherine weaved through the crowd at The Annex. Tables and tents had been set up for the many vendors.

Crafts and spices.

Jewelry and more.

Some of it was garbage, but some of it was interesting. Which was exactly why Catherine had wanted to come.

The first and only time she had been to The Annex, Catherine had found some of the coolest and most interesting pieces of jewelry. Some of them homemade, and others, just old and different. Strange and curious pieces that were a perfect fit for Catherine's odd styles and tastes. Like the conch shell bracelet Cross had made for her that she still wore every single day.

She was hoping to find something cool again today.

Catherine didn't know where Zeke had gone to. The guy disappeared shortly after they arrived. He did tell them what time they would have to leave, and where to meet him when they were ready to go.

Cross stayed close to Catherine as they navigated the growing crowd. Their fingers stayed woven together while the melting pot of people and vendors practically swallowed them whole. People watching was just as interesting to Catherine as finding one of her treasures.

"Do you know what you're looking for?" Cross asked.

Catherine eyed a table full of jarred jams. The bright red ones looked sweet. The dark-eyed woman sitting behind the jams smiled at her.

"Not until I find it," Catherine said.

Cross laughed. "This could take a while, then."

"Yep."

"Let me guess ... that's the fun part."

Catherine grinned widely. "Yep."

"I mean, as long as you're having fun, Catherine."

She squeezed his fingers woven with her own. "I always have fun with you, Cross."

He smirked, and pulled her in closer to his side. For a while, the two simply stayed like that and watched the crowd of people moving around The Annex.

"All right," Cross finally said, tugging Catherine into the crowd, "let's find you something amazing, babe."

He already had found something amazing for her.

Him.

He just didn't know it.

The Advice

Cross POV

Fuck Zeke and his doctor's appointment.
Cross checked his watch, and then the row of cars in the pick-up line of the Academy. He preferred driving home with Zeke, but that wasn't going to happen today. Rick—the enforcer who regularly worked Cross's last nerve—was nowhere to be found.
Dick.
Given all the shit Rick pulled on Cross just to make his life a living hell, he didn't doubt that making him wait today was a purposeful move. Something else for Cross to add to the growing pile of why he hated that man.
It might have made the wait easier if Catherine was with Cross, but even she was doing something else today. With one of her friends, likely. Usually she had to wait a little while after school, too. He considered pulling out his phone and texting her. Maybe she would come and keep him company.
Instead, Michel Marcello sat down beside Cross on the rock wall. Catherine's older brother looked over at him.
"Do you ever wear the school jacket?" he asked.

Cross scoffed. "No."

"Why?"

"It's fucking ugly."

"It's a blazer, man. It looks like a blazer."

"Listen, if they wanted me to wear the jacket, they'd make it in leather. Black, preferably. With no school emblem on it."

Michel nodded. "So, basically what you're wearing right now."

"Yep."

"Is that the kind of bullshit you're feeding my sister, too?"

Cross leaned back, and used his hands to support his weight. Eyeing the older teenager from the side, Cross considered how he wanted to answer that.

"Is this supposed to be one of those chats where you try to scare the hell out of me, or something?"

Michel smirked. "Would it work?"

The guy was a couple of years older than Cross. Maybe two inches taller—for now. Still, size had never mattered much to him, or made a difference when it came to breaking somebody's face. They all went down the same.

"Nope," Cross finally replied.

"Didn't think so."

"Why's that?"

Michel shrugged. "That attitude of yours is pretty well known, is all."

"Good."

The more his reputation made the rounds, the less problems he would have. Cross considered that a win, really.

"Thought you might come see me, though," Michel said.

"Why? I'm not interested in anything you're selling, Michel."

It was pretty well known around the Academy that Catherine's brother could get anybody anything they needed by way of drugs. Before Michel, it had been the guy's cousin, John.

"No, I guess you get all your shit supplied by Zeke, huh?"

Cross cocked a brow. "The only thing Zeke supplies me is the occasional phone, thanks. Assuming makes an ass out of you and me. Or haven't you heard that before?"

Michel rolled his eyes. "Come on, Donati. I know the crowd you run with, and the things they do. I've seen you at the Academy parties. We all know what I'm there to do, and why everybody else shows up."

Okay, now Cross was starting to get pissed off. He certainly wasn't a saint, considering some of the stunts he pulled, but he didn't like what Michel was implying, either.

"Listen, Michel," Cross said, "I've got no need to hide or lie about the shit I do. So, if I say I didn't do something, then I didn't fucking do it. Got it?"

Michel stayed quiet for a long while. Cross took the chance to once again check the long line of cars in the pick-up lane. Rick was still nowhere to be seen.

"As long as you keep my little sister away from that kind of shit, too," Michel said.

"You know, that kind of sounded threatening."

Michel chuckled, and pushed off the wall to land to his feet. "Well, that's because I meant for it to, Cross."

"I look out for Catherine."

"You better."

"You do realize that I'm not at all scared of you, right?"

Michel turned to face Cross again, and all his seriousness was back in a blink. "It's not really me that you've got to be afraid of, man. Remember that."

"There a point to this?"

"Like I said, I know who you are, the shit you've been known to do, and the crowd you like to run with. I just want to make sure it's clear that you know Catherine can't get mixed up in any of that kind of stuff."

"Right, because she's such an angel."

The halo was only held up by devil's horns.

"Didn't say she was, no," Michel replied easily.

Cross waved a hand to brush this whole conversation off. "Thanks for the chat and all, but I'm not really interested in talking more to you now."

Michel shook his head. "That attitude will get you nowhere with my father."

"He anything like you?"

"Worse."

Huh.

Cross had yet to meet Catherine's father face-to-face, but he heard and knew enough about Dante Marcello to know the man was all business. He apparently didn't have a lot of patience, either. Something that didn't bode well for Cross, given his nature.

Michel looked to Cross. "You got any questions for me?"

"What, like advice?"

"I guess."

"Not really."

"Suit yourself," Michel said.

Then, Cross had a thought.

"Wait," he said.

Michel slowly turned back around, and lifted a single brow. "Yeah?"

"When is Catherine's birthday, and what does she like?"

The Talk

Cross POV

"Cross, take a walk with me."

To another teenage boy, those words might have sent him running for the hills. To Cross, it kind of sounded like a challenge.

There was probably something wrong with him.

Dante Marcello stood tall and formidable in the kitchen entryway, waiting on Cross. The man's wife continued her work at the stove like she hadn't heard a thing.

Catherine's wide eyes turned on him where they both sat at the table. He pushed up out of his seat, and shot her a smirk. No need for her to worry, after all. Her father wasn't actually going to do anything to him. Maybe *try*. Although, even that was unlikely, considering his father knew where he was.

Nobody in the business of the mafia wanted to start a street war over something stupid like a teenage boy dating somebody's daughter.

Cross peeked at Dante. The man gave him a look before he turned on his heel with a wave for Cross to follow over his shoulder. He didn't say or do anything else, and he didn't look back at Cross once as they headed through the hallways of the large home. Complete silence echoed except for their footsteps hitting against hardwood floor.

Okay.

So maybe *this* man would start a street war over someone dating Catherine.

Cross still held out hope.

What the hell else did he have going for him at the moment? Arrogance was his best friend. Even when that friend did nothing but cause him problems.

Dante navigated the halls of the large home while Cross continued walking behind him, and stared at his back. When they came to the back staircase, Cross expected them to go up a level. He knew that's where Dante's office was situated in the house. Instead, Dante went down the stairs.

Cross followed silently.

Finally, Dante spoke once they were down in a cold, gray room that looked like storage. The man opened one door, and waved toward the darkness. "Go on in, Cross, and have a seat."

"Somebody going to jump out at me or something?"

Dante chuckled. "It's not the monsters you can't see that you need to be concerned about, kid."

All right.

Cross noticed something odd as he passed the door Dante was still holding open for him. The fact the man needed to hold it open or else it looked like it would slam shut was one thing. Like it was heavy as hell.

Also, it had to be at least six inches thick. All steel.

Cross blinked, realizing something else.

Soundproof, likely.

The stupid part inside his brain that literally didn't know what the taste of his own fear was shrugged it off. The smaller part of his brain that knew something wasn't right told him to back away slowly and head upstairs.

Dante was behind him.

Cross wasn't going *anywhere*.

"Take a seat," Dante repeated.

Cross stared into darkness. "Where?"

"Go in."

He took a couple of small steps into the room. Behind him, Dante followed and allowed the large, heavy metal door to slam closed behind him. The sound rattled Cross's bones, for fuck's sake.

Then, a switch was flipped, and a too-bright, bare bulb overhead lit up the space. Cross blinked rapidly to adjust his eyes to the sudden change, and take in whatever he could about the strange room.

Cement walls stared back at him. No windows. No other doors. No tables, boxes, or other things. Just four cement walls, and two folding chairs set up in the middle of the room. He wasn't fucking claustrophobic or anything, but the size of the room sure made him feel like he could be after today.

"Sit," Dante repeated.

Cross shot a look at the man, but did as he was told. Once he was finally seated, Dante moved to take the only other available chair in the room. For a long while, the two simply stared at each other, and said nothing.

Across from Cross, the man crossed his left ankle over his right knee, and offered a smile. Not a warm one, mind you, but a cold smile. Like he had Cross exactly where he wanted him or something.

Dante Marcello was a little infamous in the world of Cosa Nostra. Everywhere Cross went with his father or Wolf, Dante's name was always said with a great air of respect, or a heavy dose of fear.

Sitting across from Cross like he was, looking like the man did, he could certainly understand why some would have that impression of the Cosa Nostra boss. The thing about Cross, though?

He didn't show fear.

Even when he felt it.

"You know," Cross said, leaving his statement open and hanging.

Dante looked up from the Rolex watch on his wrist. "What's that, Cross? Tell me what you *know*."

"I was thinking that if you had a gun to sit there and clean, this whole thing would be the biggest cliché. That's just me, though."

"That so?"

Cross shrugged. "Kind of."

"I suppose I could have gotten a gun down here, had I wanted to. There are no guns in my house at the moment, however."

"No?"

That was surprising. His house was full of hidden, and plainly unhidden, guns. Almost all belonged to his father, for obvious reasons.

"Raid on my house last year," Dante said. "Another illegal weapon in my house could get me fifteen years behind bars."

"Oh."

"Shitty nature of the business, Cross." Dante waved a finger high, and circled it. "That is why the house is so well protected by men, though, if you wondered about that."

"Not really."

But it was good to know.

For a long while, Dante eyed him again without saying anything. In a way, it unnerved Cross. He hated being watched like some kind of bug that needed to be destroyed.

"You don't like me, do you?" Cross asked.

Dante chuckled. "What makes you think that?"

"The fact I'm seeing Catherine, and I have a dick."

A single eyebrow cocked high from the man in the other chair.

Cross just shrugged again.

"You know, I remember what it was like to be your age," Dante said quietly. "All pissed off at the world twenty-four seven, finally figuring out what sex was and not knowing how to satisfy it, and acting foolish all the while."

"Not sure that's how I feel about anything, actually."

Not at the moment, anyway.

Cross didn't say that out loud.

"All teenage boys are the same," Dante replied. "And they all think with the same head. We both know it's not the one on your shoulders."

Whatever.

Cross glanced around, taking in the strange room again. "We couldn't have had this conversation somewhere a little less cement-y? Like an office, or something? Pretty sure you could have said the same things to me."

"Mmm, sure," Dante said, smiling in that cold way again. "Except this room is the only room in the house with twelve-inch thick concrete walls, and a six-inch thick metal door. No one can hear a thing in here, Cross. You could be standing right outside of the door, and hear nothing inside."

Dante laughed, and pointed at the wall behind Cross, saying, "And that wall right there? Behind that wall is my wife's wine cellar. The east wall? A storage room. Useless rooms, really. We don't use them, and guests certainly aren't allowed inside them. However, even if they could get inside them, they still wouldn't hear you screaming in here. Get me?"

Cross swallowed the nerves building in his throat. "Yeah, I got you."

"Let me make something clear between us, Cross." Dante folded his arms over his chest, and relaxed in the chair. "I don't for one second think that my daughter is old enough to be dating anyone, but certainly not a boy like you."

"What kind of boy am I?"

Dante pursed his lips, and blew out a heavy sigh. "A boy that gets to grow up a little faster than other boys. Fair?"

"Sure."

"However, my wife thinks Catherine can make her own choices, and so, you are one of those choices."

"Not such a bad choice, considering."

Dante hummed under his breath. "That depends on who you ask."

"Nobody asked—I just said it."

"You really don't have an understanding of respect or fear, do you?"

Cross shrugged. "I understand both."

"Then do you understand how to put them to use? Because now

would be a great time to start working on that."

"I know the only kind of respect that fear breeds is contempt."

Dante tipped his head to the side. "That so?"

"That's what my step-father always says."

"Is that why he raises you with so little rules and boundaries that you don't understand the concept of respecting him, or giving respect when a man like me asks for it?"

Cross matched Dante's posture with his arms folded over his chest, and leaned back in the chair. "Why do you assume I don't respect Calisto?"

"I think his methods of parenting are a little lax, and it has led to a young man that is very exasperating. You, I mean."

"That's funny."

"What is?"

"That you think that," Cross said, smirking. "I respect my step-father more than anyone. Not quite as much as my ma, but ... Italians, you know."

Dante let out another one of those harsh sighs. "Your father said you had something to ask me, Cross. Go ahead and do so."

Ah, yeah.

The dance.

"So, you can tell me no?" Cross asked.

"You don't know that's what I'll say."

Cross gestured at the room, and then between them. "I have a pretty good idea."

"That smart mouth of yours is going to get you killed someday."

"Calisto says the same thing. I'm still here, though."

"Shame he hasn't somehow rid you of the impulse to talk out of turn, yet," Dante muttered. "Ask me what you wanted, Cross."

"I thought Catherine might like to go to winter formal with me. *If that's okay with you.*"

Dante lifted an eyebrow in a high arch like he was considering Cross's words. "If you ever touch my daughter without her permission, or take from her what she does not give you, I will strip your bones out of your body one by one in this room. I will do it while Catherine sits upstairs and eats dinner with the rest of her family. When I am done, I will mail pieces of you to your mother and father each day while they search for you. Do you understand me?"

Cross nodded. "Yeah, I hear you."

"You may ask my daughter to winter formal." Dante scrubbed his hands together, and added, "While we're at this, let's talk about the rules of my house."

"Which are what?"

"Doors stay open when you are alone with my daughter. Respect for my wife and me is a must. Do not behave foolishly here. Understood?"

"Sure."

Dante waved a hand as if to tell Cross he was dismissed. Cross almost made it to the door when Dante spoke again.

"Do work on the respect thing, Cross. It'll be beneficial for you in the long run. Especially in this business."

Maybe.

But probably not.

The Restaurant

Dante POV

Dante's arm struck out and knocked several overturned chairs piled on a table to the floor. It didn't help his anger a whole hell of a lot, but it felt fucking good for a minute. That's what mattered most to him.

A sigh echoed behind him as one of his two brothers stopped to pick up the chairs. Giovanni, apparently. Lucian followed behind Dante and started talking instead. He did his best to ignore his older brother. He didn't need goddamn sense talked to him right then—he had every right to be pissed. That's what he was going to be.

The up and coming restaurant currently looked like it was ready to be torn down, given the shape it was in. Covered tables and more chairs were piled high in one corner. The floor had been ripped up a couple of days ago to prepare for the stone tiles going in before the week was out. Open holes in the ceiling had bare wires hanging from them where the light fixtures would eventually go.

Another month, maybe, and the place would be in business. Another property and business to add to the Marcello profile.

It had also been the only place that wasn't a dirty warehouse—no thank you—where Dante knew would be empty. A place he could use for a little bit to get this nonsense over with, and not be noticed.

"Teenagers *do* have sex," Lucian said.

For the tenth time.

Dante rolled his eyes upward. "I swear, if you fucking say that again, I will punch you in the throat, Lucian."

Giovanni had finally caught up with them, too. "He's got a point."

"I don't care."

"Don't you think it's a little strange how in every other aspect of your life," Lucian said, "you are calm and collected, and then in walks your daughter."

Dante hesitated in his step, and turned fast to face his brothers. So fast, that the two of them almost bumped into him. "And what the hell is that supposed to mean?"

"I kind of thought it was self-explanatory," Giovanni said.

Lucian gestured at their younger brother. "What he said."

"What, like *because* it's my daughter, I automatically get raging pissed?"

"Yeah, like that, Dante."

"And *you* don't?" he asked Lucian.

"I have *three* daughters," Lucian reminded him. "Only two of which have dated. Cella is a bit too young at fifteen, but here we are, and I don't get much of a say. I know both of my older girls have—at times—stayed out too late, dated boys I hated, and have probably had sex. Jordyn keeps up on that stuff, and fills me in as necessary. Do you know how I know they've probably done that?"

"Because your wife tells you?"

"Nope," Lucian murmured. "Because they're teenagers."

"It's what we all did," Giovanni added.

Lucian jerked a thumb in Giovanni's direction. "Truth."

"It's not about the fucking *sex*," Dante snarled.

Okay.

It was a *little* about the sex.

Just a tiny bit.

But not all.

Sure, Dante thought Catherine was too young to be physical with boys, but he realized that wasn't realistic, either. If she felt ready for sex, and Catrina *really* seemed to think their daughter understood what she was doing, then he would have to deal with it.

Not like it, though.

Just deal.

"Are you sure it's not about the fact you found out she's having sex?" Lucian asked. "Because it sounds like it is, Dante."

Giovanni tipped his head in Lucian's direction. "What he said—also because I remember when you laughed to me about catching Michel in the pool when he was fifteen with a girl, and yeah. Laughed, man."

He had done that.

Fuck.

"It's not about the sex!" Dante spun on his heel, and headed for the back office. His brothers followed behind silently. "And for the fucking record, Michel got in shit for that stunt."

"Yes, another birds and the bees talk."

Giovanni snorted. "A month later, you got a warning from the school because a teacher saw him and a girl get into a car, and skip for a day. Pretty sure they weren't going shopping, or out for ice-cream."

"Shut your face, Gio."

"Just saying."

Inside the office, Dante paced. Lucian closed the door after a minute, and waited his brother out. Giovanni stayed close to the door.

"Listen, I have to head out pretty soon," he said.

Lucian looked to their younger brother. "What, not going to stay and watch the show?"

"Cal is my friend, and believe it or not, I actually kind of like his kid."

"So does he, and that's probably the only reason Cross is still alive."

Dante agreed, but then went back to pacing.

"You good?" Giovanni asked.

Lucian shrugged. "I got it, no worries."

Giovanni said something to Dante—he wasn't really listening—and then headed out of the office, but not before slamming the door. It took another three minutes before Dante felt relatively calm enough to speak again.

"Okay, so it's a little bit about the sex," he told his brother.

Lucian perched on the edge of a dusty desk. "All right."

"But there's never going to be an *old enough* for me, Lucian. She's always going to be too young, or whatever. I can't correlate my daughter and … that. None of that. It's too much in here." Dante waved a finger at his head. "Get what I mean?"

"Sure."

"Give me something more than *sure*, Lucian!"

"Someday, you're going to have to get over that, Dante. I don't know what else to tell you. What, are you going to spend the rest of her teenage life with your head stuck in the sand—is that what kind of father you want to be with her?"

"What?"

"Instead of raging about the fact she's doing something most teenagers do—including us, when we were younger—try *talking* to her. Try asking questions. And not ignorant ones, man. Not questions that make her feel judged or like she has to hide shit. Actual real, honest questions."

Dante cleared his throat. "Like what?"

"Like, is she safe? Is he respectful? Those kinds of questions mean you give a shit, and they don't present the confusion and anger you might be feeling. Get it?"

"Yeah, okay." Dante scrubbed a hand down over his face, and glanced away. "It's a lot about him, though."

"The anger, you mean?"

"That kid, Lucian, he's so fucking disrespectful. He doesn't get the fire he plays with, you know what I mean? His father just lets him do whatever the hell he wants, and now he's this arrogant little shit that could probably use today to knock him down a peg or two."

"But mostly it's because Catherine's intimate with him."

Dante shrugged.

He was done with the façade.

"Not every teenager can be raised the same way, and parents can't expect the same result," Lucian said. "Look at me with John—Giovanni with Andino. You and Michel. All three of us have taken entirely different approaches with our sons, and most of us have come out with similar respectful, decent young men."

Dante eyed Lucian. "We both know why John is a special case, and why he's a little difficult."

"His Bipolar disorder doesn't always give him a pass, Dante."

"No, I know, I just meant … No, I was giving him a pass."

"Don't do that with my son. It will not help him to excuse some of his behavior." Lucian folded his arms over his chest, adding, "But look at Andino. He was raised with little to no rules, and Gio let him run and do whatever the hell he wanted. Maybe because that's what Gio knew he needed way back when—time to figure out his shit, and the freedom to do it without judgment."

"I don't think Cross and Calisto Donati are the same as Andino and Giovanni."

"Except you don't know that, and Cross is not your son, Dante. You should allow Calisto the same respect you have given to Gio or me with our boys—take a step back, and mind your business."

Dante might have been the boss of their family, but he still—for the most part—allowed his brothers to speak openly and freely about anything they wanted with him. Forcing them to hold their opinions back had never done him any good.

Plus, it just wasn't them.

They wouldn't be his *brothers*.

"Still want to scare him a little bit," Dante said. "I'm still kind of pissed."

Lucian nodded. "All right."

His brother pulled out a gun, and waved it. "Since you don't keep one on you a lot of the time, you can use mine. When I hand it over, it'll be empty of bullets."

Dante cocked a brow. "Hmm."

"Remember, though, he is just a young man. Same as we were—we made stupid decisions, too. Slept with girls whose fathers hated us. Acted recklessly. Did dumb things. Why do you expect him to be different?"

"Because it's *my* daughter."

"Yeah, I figured." Lucian waved a finger at his temple as if to call Dante crazy. "You've got a while before they get here. Go grab a drink at the bar down the street or something."

"Really?"

"It might take the edge off."

Dante doubted it, but he went anyway.

Dante strolled across the restaurant with his hands shoved deep into the pockets of his slacks. The drink hadn't really helped to take the edge off, but his rage had ebbed.

A bit, not a lot.

It likely wouldn't help.

Outside the business, he had seen Calisto's SUV parked. At least his guests of honor had finally made it. One half of Dante had his mind on what he was doing right now, and another part was on the talk he planned to have with his daughter when he got home.

It made for a confusing mess.

Dante headed into the office without even knocking. Lucian already had set himself on the edge of the desk like he had been before. In his hands, he toyed with the gun and bullets. He barely spared Dante's entrance a glance. Dante didn't mind.

It was all about appearances, now.

Calisto stood silent in the corner with his arms folded over his chest. He gave Dante a subtle nod, but nothing more. Really, regardless of what Dante said, he did respect the Donati boss. After all, the man had brought his son here not knowing what was going to happen to him, or what Dante might do.

The young man of the hour—Cross—sat in the middle of the office on a metal folding chair. His gaze stayed on Lucian and the gun. There wasn't fear in his eyes, Dante noticed, but some people were just good at hiding it. The fact Cross wouldn't look away from Lucian's gun said a lot that he wasn't showing physically.

The kid was not stupid.

One couldn't be in this life.

Dante moved across the room, grabbed the one other folding chair, and set it up. Right in front of Cross's chair. He made sure to turn his around, so he could straddle it and set his arms over the back. That way, Cross's gaze was only on him.

Well, apparently him and the gun.

Dante hid his smirk as Cross's attention drifted between Dante, and Lucian. A subtle shift that said he wanted to know what was going to happen with that gun, but wasn't willing to ask.

For a long while, Dante simply stared at Cross before he quietly said, "Explain yourself."

Cross cocked a brow.

Dante's irritation with the kid picked up again at the sight. Like a flash of anger spiking hot and hard in his gut. A simple show of disrespect when the kid could just *talk* like he had been told to.

Instead of giving a proper answer, Cross said, "Be specific."

Dante's jaw ached from how hard he clenched his teeth at that response. "You have very little respect for better men, Cross. Let me explain this to you, so that you understand from here on out. When a better man demands something in this life, you jump through fire to give him what he wants."

"Define better."

Cross didn't even balk after the words left his mouth. He didn't blink or flinch or *think about it*. He just opened his mouth and let stupid shit come out of it.

Too arrogant.

Too difficult.

Too cocky.

Too ... *everything*.

This boy was never going to live to see his eighteenth birthday, Dante was sure of it. Cross didn't understand how death was staring him right in the face, and was ready to pull the trigger.

Maybe he had a death wish.

Maybe he had no concept of death.

No understanding of real fear.

Dante didn't know what it was, but it irked him like nothing else. Every single little thing about Cross Donati got under his skin in the worst way. Had this boy been his son, he would have made sure the kid understood the true meaning of respect.

But he wasn't his boy.

He was someone else's son.

Dante dropped a hand, and put his palm up. "Lucian."

His brother handed over the gun without a word.

Dante put his arm back over the chair, and made sure to angle the weapon just so. It forced Cross to look down the barrel.

"One more time," Dante said. "Explain."

"*Again*, be specific."

"Calisto should genuinely worry for your life, Cross. You're too rude, too insolent, and that'll never make a good made man."

"But it will make a dead one," Lucian said from behind Dante.

Calisto cleared his throat in the corner. In the corner of his eye, Dante could plainly see how uncomfortable the man was with the scene, though he hid it well. He was probably hoping this would be some kind of wakeup call for Cross.

Who knew?

Cross didn't look away from the gun, or Dante. "If you want me to explain what happened on Friday, I don't think I need to. The school made a nice little slideshow with videos and all, Dante."

Yes, that stupid video. The principal was lucky Dante didn't decide to burn her fucking house to the ground, the bitch.

Dante opted not to say that out loud, and instead, went in a different direction.

"Don," Dante said to the kid, "or boss."

"Not mine," Cross replied.

"Cross." Calisto's warning rang out heavily.

Cross didn't reply or look away from Dante.

"No," Dante said, leaning forward, "I want you to explain to me what you would say to ever justify putting my daughter in the kind of position you did. You see, you're selfish, Cross, like most boys your age. I expect that, to an extent, but what I *demand* will always be respect. Especially for my daughter."

Cross just continued staring—blank as a piece of paper. No fear, no distress, and no discomfort. Like he didn't give a single fuck what was happening.

This kid was either crazy, or he literally did not understand genuine fear.

Dante didn't know which one it was, but both bothered him. Especially considering Cross was dating his daughter. He did not want to think about all the shit the two might get into with the way Cross behaved.

"You don't think with the head up here," Dante said, tapping Cross's forehead with the tip of the gun's barrel. Then, he clicked off the safety, racked the gun, and pointed it downward. Right at Cross's lap—at his groin, actually. "No, you're too busy thinking with the smaller head down there because that's easy gratification."

Anyone would have flinched.

Dante would have fucking flinched.

Cross just sat here, still blank.

Pissed, Dante stood, and pushed the chair away. His gun stayed pointed downward, and then he pulled the trigger. Of course, the weapon only clicked because it was empty.

Cross didn't even jump. He just stared at Dante as though he knew that was going to happen.

"Are we done?" Cross asked dryly.

Yes, they absolutely were.

Should he stay in that office for five more minutes, he was not sure what he might do to Cross Donati.

Nothing good.

"You better hope we never have to revisit this conversation, Cross, or one even marginally like it," Dante said, and dropped the gun in Cross's lap. "If you ever put my daughter in a positon like that again, this will end far differently for you. Frankly, we shouldn't have to worry about this again anyway because you're going to keep your distance from Catherine from here on out."

"All right," Cross said.

One more slight to add to a growing pile, Dante knew.

"All right, *what?*" Dante asked sharply.

Cross stood from the chair, looked Dante in the eye, and smirked.

He *smirked*.

Dante had all he could not to hit the kid. It probably wouldn't have made a difference anyway.

"All right, *nothing*," Cross replied, still smirking.

Then, the young man was out of the office. Lucian blew out a heavy breath when the door slammed shut, and even Calisto made a harsh sound in the corner.

"That kid is going to get himself killed," Dante warned Calisto.

The Donati boss nodded. "You know, that's very likely."

"And yet, here we are, Calisto."

"Seems so."

Dante pointed at the door. "Make sure that never happens again."

The Talk

Catherine POV

Catherine placed her hands to her knees, and pushed down in an effort to make them stop bouncing. It didn't work. Instead of just her legs trembling with her nerves, now, her arms shook, too.

Across the living room, her mother's sharp gaze watched her from over the magazine. Catherine avoided meeting her mother's stare at all costs. It was just easier this way—it made it seem like she wasn't open for conversation.

Apparently, Catrina didn't care much about that.

"You know," her mother said, "I assumed you were either having sex, or you were … doing other things, but I wasn't sure until today. Why didn't you talk to me?"

Catherine shrugged. "I didn't have anything to say, Ma."

Catrina lifted one perfectly manicured brow high. "Nothing?"

"No."

"For how long?"

Catherine made a face, and continued avoiding her mother's gaze. "A couple of months."

"Around your birthday?"

"Do we have to talk about this?"

Catrina laughed dryly. "Catherine, do you think you're ready to be having sex if you're not capable of having a mature conversation about everything?"

Catherine's molars ached when she grinded her teeth. Her mother had a good point, but that didn't exactly mean she wanted to admit it.

"We've talked about sex before," Catherine said quietly.

"We've talked about logistics, safety, and things, sure. We've never talked about intimate things, or whatever else."

"Shouldn't those things be private?"

"Should they?" Catrina asked back. "You're sixteen. I think it would be inconsiderate of me not to be concerned about things, Catherine."

"Well, what kind of things, Ma?"

"Well, for one, do you enjoy intimacy?"

Catherine's face reddened. *"Ma."*

"It's a simple question. If sex or any kind of intimacy is traumatic in some way—be that it hurts, or is scary, or even uncomfortable—that's something to consider. My question remains the same, *dolcezza*."

"It's …"

"Hmm?"

"Good," she finally settled on saying.

It didn't necessarily describe how wonderful and amazing it felt, or how Cross treated her with careful hands and more, but it was enough. She was not going into more detail where that was concerned.

Some things *should* be private.

"Good," Catrina deadpanned.

Catherine peered over at her mother, and smiled a little. "It's really good, Ma. He's … considerate? Yeah, that's a good way to say it."

Catrina pursed her lips. "Okay."

"What else?"

"Did you feel pressured—before, now … anytime?"

"No," Catherine rushed to say. "Never."

"How often do you feel a need to be intimate in a place like school?"

Yep …

There it was.

Catherine knew it was coming.

All over again, her face reddened.

"That was the first time," she admitted.

"I take it you understand—"

"How stupid it was? Yeah, I got that, Ma."

"I bet." Catrina sighed, adding, "but I was going to say, I take it you understand how irresponsible it was."

"That, too."

Catrina tossed the magazine aside. "See, sex can be wonderful, Catherine. And no one should ever make you feel ashamed or put down because you enjoy sex. Whether some of us in this house like to admit it or not, you're just like every other human coming into adulthood. You feel the same things—need and want the same things. Some of those things are intimate and physical in nature. You may not be at an age where it's easier to accept what you do, but pretending that you don't do them certainly won't help."

"Daddy's very angry at me."

"Yes, he is." Catrina shrugged, and said, "Truth be told, at first it was probably the shock of realizing his daughter isn't the same little girl who used to refuse to wear anything but a tutu. After that shock wore off, his anger changed direction, and now it's what you did, and where you did it."

"Yeah, I know."

"He's due his anger, Catherine. You have to understand why he has it."

Catherine chewed on her inner cheek before asking, "And what about you, Ma?"

"Hmm?"

"The anger he has with you for not telling him that you thought I was having sex, or for putting me on birth control without talking to him about it. Do you understand why he's angry?"

Catrina smiled. "I understand—I don't agree. Therein lies the difference between our circumstances with your father at the moment. You were in the wrong. He only thinks I was in the wrong."

"Don't you think he might not have been so angry or shocked had you talked to him about ... me and sex?"

"Probably."

"But you still think—"

"That he needs to climb down from his high horse, or I will knock him down from it, yes."

Perfect.

Catherine could already tell it was going to be difficult to live in her house for the unforeseeable future. Definitely not fun, all things considered. Her parents were two of the most stubborn people she knew, and neither one of them backed down from a fight.

She didn't want to be the reason they were fighting.

Yet, here she was.

Being exactly that.

Yeah.

Perfect.

Not five minutes later, Catherine heard the roar of a familiar engine. Her father's car. All over again, humiliation filled her to the brim, and her heart felt heavy.

It was only made worse when her father came into the house, found her in the living room, and said nothing.

No, he only stared at her.

Disappointment looked back.

"Catherine," her father said.

She looked up at him. "Yes, Daddy?"

"There's only two things I want to know at the moment."

"Okay."

"Are you being safe?" he asked.

Catherine's gaze darted to her mother, and then back to Dante. "Yes."

"Have you ever felt like you had to do something that you did not want to do?"

"No," Catherine said quickly.

"All right." Her father waved a hand at the doorway. "Go to your room."

She barely made it out of the living room before the yelling started between her parents. She didn't come out of her room until morning.

7

The Run

Cross POV

Whiskey burned all the fucking way down. Cross tipped that bottle up and took another long swig. The noise of the house party got louder and louder until it was nothing more than an irritation in his ear.

Drunk, and with his vision swimming, Cross weaved through the people. A couple called his name, but he ignored them altogether.

Right then, he just needed to get *away*.

That's why he'd left his fucking house in the first place. Why had Zeke invited so many damn people?

The heat crawled beneath his leather jacket in an almost smothering way. He could feel the thumping in his throat—signaling something bad was coming. He moved a little bit faster, if only because he didn't want his friend to have to clean a mess.

Cross barely made it through the backdoor before he lost his lunch all over the stone tiles. Whiskey burned coming up the same way it did going down, but it didn't taste half as fucking good this time around.

"Oh, shit!"

Someone else laughed.

"You okay, man?"

Cross blinked, and put his hands to his knees. He couldn't remember how old he was the last time he had drank enough liquor to make him sick. Maybe fourteen, or thirteen.

"Fuck," he hissed, spitting to the ground.

The laughter of the people gathered outside only grated on his nerves even more. He didn't like to make a spectacle of himself. It just wasn't what he did.

Yet, there he was.

Being laughed at.

Being watched.

Fuck.

All he wanted right then was *not* to feel. To be numb inside and out. To breathe, but not feel like it took effort with every single breath.

He didn't want to hurt.

Not in his heart, or his soul.

He only needed to be numb.

"Here, man," somebody said.

Cross looked up to find one of Zeke's older friends standing next to him. The guy with the gray-blue eyes held out a smoldering joint. The heady scent of weed made his stomach feel even heavier all at once.

The guy chuckled like he could see Cross's disgust.

"Yeah, I know," he said. "This strain has a strong smell, but it does wonders for making nausea go away, or just making you feel better. It's yours if you want it."

Cross smacked his mouth.

Vomit still lingered there.

He eyed the joint, and swallowed hard.

Drugs weren't usually his thing. Sometimes he'd take a couple of hits off a joint when he was at a party, and Zeke was looking out for him. That was really it, though.

He didn't make it a regular thing.

"I don't want to think or feel anything at all," Cross said.

The guy nodded. "Yeah, it's good for that, too."

That was all Cross needed to hear. He snagged the joint, and took the first drag. He didn't cough or choke, and instead, chased the smoke back with another drink of burning whiskey.

Numbness was the goal.

He needed it.

Something shifted beside Cross, and his drug and drink induced brain was slow to react. He should have been down for the count—a foggy memory of Zeke pulling him off the couch and guiding him to the bedroom lingered in the back of his mind.

Wasn't he in bed?

Soft.

Warm.

Comfortable.

Yeah, he was definitely in bed.

Another shift beside him, and Cross finally opened his eyes. He glanced over; his vision still swam with a high and drunk that had not quite let him go, yet. He couldn't have been in bed for very long. He could still hear the party going on outside the bedroom.

Music.

People laughing.

Someone shouting.

All those thoughts registered to Cross first, and the woman staring at him registered second. He stared at her for a long while wondering what in the hell she was doing in the bedroom with him. He felt her hands first—gliding over his bare chest, and then beneath his boxer-briefs.

Zeke had made him get undressed.

Puke on your clothes, man.

"What the—"

"Hey," the girl said.

Then, she was on him.

Cross barely even got a word in, or understood what happened, and the chick was in his lap, and looking down at him. Her hands stroked his dick, and because he couldn't control the reaction of his body when somebody just rubbed on him enough, he hardened.

"Like that, do you?"

No.

She was pretty enough, sure.

Blonde.

Brown-eyed.

Not Catherine.

All things that worked in her favor.

Cross was still fucked up—way too messed up to be doing this. And who the hell just came into a bedroom and climbed on somebody that was sleeping?

"Get off," Cross said.

"Don't be like that."

Her fingers tightened.

"Besides," she added, "I think you like it."

"Get *off*."

Somewhere in his hazy mind, shit became clear.

This was how easy it could be for somebody to do shit like this. To take advantage. To hurt, and think it was okay.

It pissed him off, and made him sick at the same time.

"Get the fuck off," Cross snarled.

His words were still slurred.

His strength was not up to par.

He still shoved the girl away from him. So hard, in fact, that she fell off the side of the bed. The thump cleared his foggy brain in an instant. The haze wasn't gone, but he didn't feel entirely high or drunk anymore.

The hangover tomorrow was going to be a bitch.

"Asshole," the girl said.

"Get out."

Cross rolled over in the bed, and yanked the blankets up over his head.

"And lock the fucking door," he added in a mumble.

"Cross, your phone is ringing again."

"Leave it," Cross said.

Zeke still picked up the device and checked the home page. "It's your father."

"Fuck, man, I said to leave it."

"Shit, all right. Relax."

Cross went back to cleaning the nine-millimeter. Zeke never took proper care of his guns, and it drove Cross crazy.

"Dad called me a couple times today," Zeke said.

"Yeah."

"Asked about you."

"Yeah," Cross repeated dryly.

"Wanted to know when you were going to head home."

"*Yeah.*"

"Cross," Zeke said quietly.

Cross looked up from the gun, and found his friend was staring him down. "What?"

"You've been here a week."

"And I might be here for another week." Cross shrugged. "Unless you've got something to say about that, I mean."

"You know you're welcome to stay here any fucking time you want, man."

"All right."

"Except my father said your mother is worried, and Calisto is two seconds away from sending somebody after your ass to take you home. He knows where you are—that's probably the only reason he hasn't done anything yet."

"Probably," Cross agreed.

"That's all you've got to say?"

No.

Yes.

Really, Cross didn't know.

He didn't know anything.

At the moment, his entire life felt like one big fucking mess. A shit show. Catherine was … gone. That's what he knew. And with her went a piece of him. A giant chunk of his heart that was supposed to be hers because he was fucking stupid. Like an idiot, he had handed over another piece of himself without even thinking about what that might mean.

He didn't consider she might hurt him again.

Because *love*.

Love was bullshit.

Not a lie, no.

It couldn't be a lie when he felt it. He knew it was real. Every single part of him loved Catherine Marcello. That didn't mean he had to like it a whole lot right now. It certainly didn't feel very damn good.

So yeah.

Love was garbage.

"You know," Zeke said, "you didn't really tell me what happened. You just showed up, got drunk for three days, smoked up in between, and slept a lot. I mean, today's the first day you actually got up and did something. And all you did was bitch about my gun and clean it, man. You don't … talk."

"Is that what you want, or something?"

"What?"

"To talk about my feelings? Menstruate once a month? Grow vaginas? The way I feel isn't up for conversation, Zeke."

His friend just shook his head. "Christ, you are such an asshole sometimes. You know I just want to help, right? That's it."

Helping him would be to leave him alone. Or, to be quiet. Helping wouldn't be asking questions, or making Cross feel like shit all over again. Helping was a lot of things, but it wasn't anything Zeke was offering at the moment.

Cross didn't tell his friend any of those things.

Instead, he said, "Catherine broke up with me. I don't want to talk about it—there's nothing to say, but I don't want to be at home right now. I needed to be somewhere else. Here I am."

Or rather, he couldn't be home.

Cross needed some time. He didn't know what for, really. Maybe to recharge, or to get shit straight in his head. Something ... He just needed time away from being the *principe*. Time away from being his mother and step-father's son, and his sister's big brother. Time away from a place that constantly reminded him of Catherine for a million and one different reasons.

Maybe then when he went back, shit would be okay.

Except it probably wouldn't be.

So was his fucking life.

"I forgot to tell you something," Zeke said.

Cross grumbled under his breath, and then asked, "What now?"

"Dad's coming over today. Said he might be able to convince you it's time to go home. Thought you might like a heads up."

Zeke cocked a brow when Cross glanced at his friend. He heard Zeke's unspoken words—the ones he had to read between the damn lines.

Here's your chance to go if you need or want to before he gets here.

"Got another couch for me to sleep on for the week?" Cross asked.

Zeke shrugged. "I can find you somewhere."

"Yeah, do that."

"I should warn you, though ..."

"What?"

"Dad said if you keep this shit up, Calisto might just send someone out to hunt you down and bring you home anyway."

Cross made a dismissive noise under his breath. "He can try."

"Wake your ass up, *principe*! I know you're in here."

Cross groaned, and yanked the blankets higher over his head. He wasn't even sure whose fucking couch he was sleeping on that morning—it had been changing from day to day. Whoever had a party, or whoever invited him to stay.

He wasn't fucking picky.

He just didn't want to go home.

"Cross, don't make me come further into that house."

"Hey ... hey, man, wake up."

Somebody shook Cross's shoulder hard enough to wake him from the hungover stupor he was currently in. The blinding sunlight coming in from the windows told him it was well into the day. The sight of the light instantly made his stomach want to revolt.

Too much liquor.

Too much of everything else.

Fuck his life.

"All right, Cross, don't say I didn't fucking warn you."

"Man, get up before that guy tears my fucking house apart."

Cross looked up at the guy standing over him—Tim, Jim, or fuck, who knew? "Who?"

"*Principe*, your step-father is waiting outside. Make it easy on me, or I have permission to stuff your ass in the trunk of my car. Compliments of the boss."

Fuck.

"Go away, Rick," Cross snarled.

Stupid ass enforcer.

The guy still wouldn't leave Cross alone.

He'd made it three weeks. Three weeks of just ... being. Alone. No responsibilities. Recharging. Getting used to being just him without Catherine.

It was not a nice place to be, he learned.

"Fuck."

That was all the guy who owned the couch said.

Then, the blanket that was covering Cross was ripped off. Cross found himself locked in a staring contest with Rick, but he refused to move.

Rick spoke first.

"Again, your step-father is outside. He says enough is enough. You've been gone long enough—not answering calls, or checking in. Scaring your mother half to death. He's done with your nonsense. Move your ass without me needing to do it, or I will personally stuff your stupid self into the trunk and drive you home. I'm sure it'll be a nice lesson for you, you spoiled little shit."

Cross glowered more.

Rick was unaffected. "Get up."

"Fuck you."

"Hard way it is, then."

Cross cocked a brow at the enforcer. "You touch me, and you *die*."

"Are you going to get up?"

"Is Cal really outside?"

"I guess you're either going to get up and find out for yourself, or I'm going to carry you out there. Which one do you want to choose?"

Cross walked himself out there.

Calisto was waiting.

Neither of them spoke for days after, though.

The Spiral

Catherine POV

"Catherine!"

Catherine ignored her mother's call, and snagged her bag from the hallway. Her shit was all over the house—discarded wherever it had fell from her hand when she was done with it. Usually that would be something that irritated her mother to no end, but lately, Catrina stopped trying to say anything at all about it.

It wasn't doing any good.

Catherine still left her shit here and there, and Catrina's yelling only fell on deaf ears. After all, she needed interest and desire to do something. Especially when it came to picking up her things, or keeping stuff clean.

Lately, Catherine had none of that.

Shrugging the bag over her shoulder, she headed down the stairs. Her mother continued calling her name, and Catherine kept ignoring her. She was almost to the front of the house when Catrina finally caught up with her.

Damn.

Almost made it.

"Catherine," her mother said one last time before Catherine had enough.

"I'm going out."

Maybe if she just told her, then Catrina would leave her alone. Her parents seem to be doing that a lot lately. As if they didn't know what to do with Catherine, or how to deal with her behavior. Even the mood swings came at the most difficult, and unknown, times.

She was up, and then she was down in the next damn minute.

Her mind could be free, clear, and good. And then the next day? She could be dark, her thoughts blackened with rage, bitterness, or hate, and her body became tired. Tired of existing, and tired of trying. A deep ache in her heart that always seemed to travel through her bones never really left, even on the good days.

But the thoughts?

Her black emotions?

Those were the very worst.

Those were what frightened her the most. She had somehow become a vision of herself that she no longer knew, and one she didn't recognize. A vision that sometimes couldn't be bothered to try, not even to brush her hair. And on other days, that same vision would be of a young woman who used makeup and fake smiles to hide tear stains, and memories that never quite let her go for very long.

She could barely stand to look in the mirror a lot of the time because who was that woman looking back at her? She didn't know who it was.

Certainly not her.

Or, it wasn't who she wanted to be.

It wasn't even close to who she used to be.

"Going where?" Catrina asked.

"Out," Catherine said.

"Catherine, the least you can do is tell me where exactly you're going to be tonight."

Was that the least she could do?

Catherine figured the least she could have done was get out of bed that day. Because hell, most times, even that was a chore she didn't want to do. And so, she had done exactly that. She was out of bed, she was talking, and being somewhat pleasant. She figured that should have been good enough for her mother, all things considered.

Catrina moved past her daughter, and blocked the front door. It wasn't like her mother to be so physical, but a lot of things had changed lately.

The biggest of those changes being Catherine herself.

"Tell me where you're going," Catrina said, "and then you can go."

"To a party," Catherine said.

"A party in the city."

"That's what I said." Catherine shrugged. "So, now you know where I'm going. I told you, like you wanted. Move, and let me go."

Catrina didn't move. "Your father doesn't want you leaving the house. You're supposed to be grounded because you snuck out three weeks ago."

"Well, Daddy isn't here, is he?"

"He will be, and what am I to tell him, then?"

Catherine stared hard at her mother, unmoved. "Honestly, Ma, I don't give a shit what you tell Daddy."

"Catty."

What did her mother want from her?

Catherine didn't know.

She didn't have anything left to give.

"Please let me go, Ma. I just need to get out of this house."

She needed to breathe.

She needed to feel something else.

She needed to do something else.

For a long while, the two women stared at each other. Neither of them said a word. A good couple of minutes passed before Catrina finally stepped to the side, and gave her daughter access to the front door.

"Be here when your father wakes up in the morning," her mother said.

Catherine agreed.

She also lied.

It was just easier.

Catherine's vision swam with all of the things in front of her. Dancing people, rooms and hallways, and the unfamiliar.

The unsafe.

After everything, she should know better than to be in a place like this, doing the things she was doing. Hadn't her rape taught her that?

It never failed.

Even in the safety of Catherine's own mind, her thoughts blamed her for what happened. Like a poison that wouldn't stop spreading, her thoughts seemed intent on never letting her forget. No matter what she did.

Alcohol made her blood thick. Weed made her mind light.

When she was drunk or high, or both at the same time, then she no longer had to feel. Nothing that would hurt her, anyway. Nothing that would lead her back down a black hole of nothingness that constantly squeezed around her heart, and her mind. A black hole that left her empty, cold, and so alone.

She should have been working. That's what she'd come here to do in the first place.

Funny ...

Catherine couldn't remember the last time she actually came to a party to deal like she was supposed to. So far, her cousins hadn't figured out a lot of the shit she was doing. Partying, and whatever else.

She knew the moment Andino or John learned that she had fallen into this abyss, the first thing they would do would be pull her back out of it.

She wasn't ready for that yet.

She didn't want to deal with that yet.

She couldn't deal with herself, yet.

Someone called her name from within the crowd of drunken teenagers, but she didn't know who. Catherine waved a hand high, figuring that would be enough.

It wasn't like she came here to talk.

She didn't get drunk to be social.

Now, she didn't want to be anything at all.

Catherine tried to remember how many times this month alone that she had gotten drunk, high, or both. It was a bigger number then she cared to admit.

It was a problem.

She knew that.

But what could she do?

How could she stop?

This was easier.

So much easier.

Catherine weaved through the people, and found her way back into the hallways. She found a staircase that let to the upstairs of a house that she didn't recognize.

Whose place was this, anyway?

Who fucking knew?

Not her.

She didn't care, either.

Catherine found one room upstairs that wasn't being used by someone else. It looked like a bedroom, not that she cared. She closed the door, and dug out the cell phone from her purse. For a long while, she only stared at the black screen.

She was too drunk, too high ...

Way too fucked up.

She should have called her father, or mother. She came here to forget and not feel, but the only thing she could think about was how bad she didn't want to be there anymore.

Funny how that worked.

She should have called someone and asked for help. It was the only thing her parents asked of her, really. They knew something was wrong, but they didn't know how to deal with it. They no longer knew how to deal with her.

Catherine understood that all too well.

She no longer knew how to deal with herself.

And worse was when she was like this, when she was so lost like this, there was only one thing she knew to do. There was only one person who could make her feel slightly better when she was like this.

Was it selfish?

Did she care?

There was only one person she cared to call. He always answered. He was always saving her. Even when she hurt him.

Cross.

9

The Save

Cross POV

Despite the thick fog of dreams keeping Cross firmly stuck in sleep, he still somehow heard the ringing of his cell phone. Faint and barely there at all, the ringing drove him from the dream, and had him peeling his eyes open to find the darkness of his bedroom staring back at him. For a split second, he wasn't even sure why he had woken up, but the phone rang again.

A familiar tune.

One meant for her.

So then, he knew …

"Shit," Cross mumbled.

Rolling over, Cross waved his hand blindly to find the phone on his nightstand. Finally, he had it in his grasp. Putting it to his ear, he buried himself back beneath the blankets as he answered the call.

"Catherine," he murmured, his voice thick with sleep.

"Cross?"

Damn.

He knew what she was going to ask before the words even left her mouth. Maybe it was the high, light way her words came out, but the whine that lingered in her tone. Catherine only sounded like that when she was drunk, or high.

He hated it when she sounded like that.

It always meant bad things.

"Are you at home?" she asked.

Cross tossed the blanket off, and scrubbed a hand down his jaw. "Yeah, in bed."

"Oh."

Soft, and unsure.

Like she was scared.

Cross hated that, too.

He could hear the thumping music in the background, and the muffled laughter of people. A door slammed, and the noise lessened in the background for a moment.

She was not at home—that much was clear.

A party, likely.

Something she had been doing far too often, lately.

"Well, okay," Catherine said, "I'll let you—"

"Where are you?"

"In the city."

Cross stared up at the ceiling of his bedroom. "Mmm, yeah, but doing what?"

"Working."

Lies.

She rarely worked when she went out, now. Catherine thought he didn't know, but he did. She was dealing more and more at school. It was concerning because it was dangerous. He didn't really get a say, though, because they weren't *something* anymore.

Not officially, anyway.

She called.

He went.

She cried.

He saved.

Like a circle that never ended.

Apparently, tonight would not be the night it ended, either.

"Give me the address," he said. "I'll be there in an hour or less."

"You don't have to."

Yeah, he did.

"I'm already out of bed, Catherine."

That was a lie, but it was only for her benefit.

Catherine whispered the address.

Cross finally got out of bed.

"I'll be there soon," he promised.

"Okay."

Cross's house was still dark and quiet when he finally got back. Only, he wasn't alone like he had been when he left.

Catherine, not as drunk or stupid as he thought she might be, stayed close to his side as they navigated the halls of the Donati home. Her fingers wove with his as they slipped into his bedroom.

He took extra care to make sure they were quiet. Sure, his parents' bedroom was one floor higher, but sometimes, all it took was a floorboard creaking to wake up Calisto.

Cross was in no way interested in explaining why Catherine was with him, how much she had been drinking, or anything else. His parents would not approve. They would tell him to send her home.

He couldn't do that.

Not when she asked to stay.

Cross barely got the bedroom door closed before Catherine was shedding her clothes. In only a bralette and panties, she crawled into his bed, and disappeared under the blankets. She did all of that without even saying a word.

He expected nothing different.

Sometimes, she was all too predictable. She just wanted him close, but not too close. She wanted to feel him near, but not too much of him.

She was up.

She was down.

Like whiplash coming for him at every fucking turn, he no longer knew how to handle it, or what to do.

Sure, he wanted to help.

He just didn't know how.

Instead, Cross did this. He went when she called, he made sure she was safe, and he kept her that way for as long as he could.

Catherine would disappear into his blankets and bed until she was ready to face the world again. Cross made sure she always had the time to do exactly that.

No matter what.

"Cross?"

Her quiet, muffled question had him crossing the bedroom.

"Yeah, babe?"

From beneath the blankets, he heard her ask, "Will you get in bed? I'm cold."

Sure, she was.

He knew what she wanted.

He kicked off his shoes, and stripped down to his boxer-briefs. Climbing into the bed, and hiding beneath the blankets like she had done, Cross found Catherine staring at him.

Maybe he understood why she did this all too often with him.

Maybe it made more sense.

The world looked nicer under here.

With only her …

It was safer.

Silently, he reached out and pulled her in tight to his body. His arms cradled around her like a cage keeping her safe, and warm.

Catherine buried her face into his chest, and let out a soft sigh. "Thanks, Cross."

Her unspoken words were far louder.

She had a problem with talking lately.

"No problem."

Questions rattled around in his mind—things he needed to ask, but could never seem to say. It wasn't like him to be so reserved with anybody, but that was the thing.

Catherine wasn't just *anyone*.

She was her.

She was his.

He wanted to know if this was the last time he would have to go pull her from some house party, but he didn't think it would be. He wanted to ask if they were ever going to get back to being them again, but was a little scared of the answer.

Her parents were probably wondering where she was. No doubt, Cross would be the one to take her home again in the morning, while at the same time, trying to avoid the burning glares Dante Marcello tossed his way.

Did she know how he felt her father's hate grow with every new morning he showed up with a hungover Catherine in his car? Did she even care at all?

It was hard to say, and he wasn't willing to ask. Sometimes, talking did no good lately when it came to Catherine.

She raged, sure.

She cried.

But actually *talking*?

No.
Not really.
Instead of saying anything, he simply held her.
She was here.
That was good enough.
"Do you still love me?"
Cross looked down to see familiar green eyes watching him. "Always."
After all, he didn't know anything different.
Only her.

Revere Era Shorts

10

The Fear

Catrina POV

Catrina hated hospitals, and yet the cold, sterile buildings had given her some of the happiest moments of her life. Lives saved, and new births. Moments of relief, or of calm and peace. Moments that stuck to the back of her mind forever like caramel—sticky and sweet.

It didn't matter, though.

Those memories were not enough to quell the coldness that slipped down her spine every time she came to this place. It was not enough to stop the dread as it drove a nail through her heart when she opened the entrance doors.

See, for every good memory that Catrina had of hospitals, five more negative ones were just as apparent in her mind.

A shame, really.

Tonight, she could add another good and bad memory to the pile. Good, of course, because her daughter's young and vibrant life had been saved. Bad, surely, because of why it needed saving in the first place.

In a chair tucked away in the corner of the hospital's waiting room, Catrina sat alone. Not by her gathered family's choice, but by her own. It was easier to process the events of the night, and to deal with her raging emotions without the others around. She knew they were worried. She could see the concern and questions staring back from the gazes of her in-laws. Yet, she still had no words to say to them.

Not yet, anyway.

She wasn't ready.

Still, they wouldn't push. She knew it.

It was one of the many good things about the Marcellos. Having spent so many years together as a tightknit group—growing and loving—they had learned to give each other space when needed.

Not every problem could be solved by talking. Not all wounds could be healed with an apology. Not all negative emotions could be stopped with a hug.

Time.

Space.

Silence.

Those things were sometimes their best friends.

Like now.

Catrina glanced down at the clipboard in her hands. More hospital forms to fill out. She should have finished with them an hour or more ago, yet here she still was, looking at unanswered questions. These were not like the medical and insurance forms she had filled out earlier when they first arrived.

The questions were different—personal and invasive.

She supposed that was why she hesitated on the answers. That, and she wasn't sure she knew the answers to some of them.

It wasn't like Catherine was currently able to answer them.

Or maybe ... just maybe, Catrina didn't want to know the answers to some of them. Hindsight was always twenty-twenty. That little fact was never more apparent to her than now. Now, when she did not want to look back at her daughter's young life, and see the red flags Catrina might have missed. The flashing lights that might have warned her this horrible night was on the horizon.

Catrina knew the signs would be there.

She had missed them. All of them.

She failed.

She failed her child.

She failed.

Catrina let out a slow breath, and looked at the forms once more.

Has the patient ever self-harmed?

Has the patient ever self-medicated?

Untreated depression?

Trauma?

Words like mental health, emotional instability, and more harsh realities stared back at Catrina. The question that stood out the most above the others also burned the very worst.

Has the patient ever attempted suicide before?

No, she wanted to write. Yet, she didn't put anything at all. How could she when she didn't know for sure, and couldn't currently ask her eighteen-year-old daughter?

How awful of a mother did it make her that she didn't know the answers? That she was scared to ask? What would Catherine say?

How would Catrina respond if her daughter did actually tell her the truth?

A while back, Catrina watched—unsure of how to help or what to do—as her daughter faded further away from them, and too far out of reach. To where, Catrina hadn't known. A dark place, surely.

Catrina saw Catherine come closer again—be vibrant and bright again. Now … this.

Now, a fresh wound on a delicate wrist. Now, a bloodstained bathroom to clean. Now, a broken young woman to somehow save from herself.

A broken heart didn't do something like this, Catrina knew.

A shattered mind did.

Hopelessness did this.

Wounded hearts did not.

"Mrs. Marcello?"

Catrina looked up to find a man peering down at her. Under his white lab coat, he wore a dress shirt, tie, and slacks. A doctor, most definitely.

"Yes?" she asked.

"I'm Doctor Powski. I was called in by the ER doctor to come down and assess your daughter's case. I understand that you and your husband have requested she be put under a seventy-two hour psych hold."

Catrina flinched. "For a suicide watch, yes."

Powski glanced around. "Is your husband nearby so we can all sit down together and discuss—"

"He stepped out."

Catrina offered no other information to the doctor. Dante wasn't handling all of this very well. What else was there to say?

"Okay," the doctor said, and then he took a seat beside hers. "First, I'll give you an update on Catherine's current state. If you would like that, of course."

"Please."

"She's stable now that she's had two blood transfusions. Her counts are looking positive, as well. She did have quite an amount of alcohol noted in her blood."

"Likely—she downed two bottles of wine."

The man nodded. "I see. Well, currently she's sedated to allow her some time to rest, and continue to get fluids through the IV. Right now, she's in a private room on this floor, but once the paperwork is signed for the seventy-two hour hold, she will be moved."

"To where?'

"Upstairs to the Psych Ward."

Again, Catrina flinched.

Still, she replied calmly, "Okay."

The doctor openly frowned. "Can I assume by your demeanor that your daughter's suicide attempt did not come as a surprise?"

"What you can assume from my demeanor is that I am a very composed woman, sir, and nothing else."

"My apologies."

Catrina swallowed her nerves, and asked, "Could I see her now?"

"Of course."

In the hospital bed, tucked beneath white blankets and sleeping, Catherine actually looked peaceful. As though she had no worries, and her life had not been hanging in the balance only a few hours earlier.

The peacefulness in Catherine's features was only an illusion, Catrina knew. As soon as the sedatives wore off, Catherine would wake up to a life that she and just tried to permanently escape from.

"I'll give you a few minutes," the doctor said from the doorway. "Then we can discuss the specifics of signing the papers for the hold."

Catrina nodded. "Thank you."

The doctor closed the door as he left until only a small slit remained. In private, with no one to witness the cracks forming in Catrina's very put together façade, the heartache finally started to show. It began with a shaky breath, and then the trembling in her hands came next. The first tear slid down her cheek as she looked upward.

Her relationship with God had always been tenuous at best. A love-hate relationship that pushed and pulled too much from her heart. A give and take where she was always the one giving—it never seemed like she ever got anything back.

That's how God sometimes works, Cat, her husband liked to say. *It's called faith. We give it to Him without question.*

Catrina didn't see it the same way. She had far, *far* too many questions for God. She didn't even know where to begin usually.

Not tonight, though.

Tonight, she knew exactly what she wanted to say.

Please, please ... give her happiness and love and little pain. Please, please ... give her those things, and I'll give you unquestioned faith and trust. Please, please ...

"Cat?"

At the sound of her husband's voice coming from the doorway behind her, Catrina quickly wiped the few tears away that had escaped. It didn't matter, though. When she turned to face Dante, he saw what she tried to hide.

He always did.

In two steps, he was with her. Holding her face in his warm hands, and dragging her close. He wiped away her second rush of tears, and kissed her lips softly.

"It'll be all right," he told her.

"Will it?"

"Eventually."

Catrina let out a weak breath. "Do you remember when she was brand new—thirty-two hours of labor and four deep stiches later?"

Dante chuckled. "Can't forget it."

"But do you remember how I felt then? After we brought her home, I mean."

"Like a baby deer walking on new legs."

Catrina sniffled, and nodded. "I didn't know what to do—how to be a mom to a brand new baby. I didn't know how to take care of her, or where to begin. I was so ... out of my element."

"First time I ever saw you struggle with something," Dante admitted. "It was strange for me, too, in that way."

"I'm back in that place again," Catrina whispered. "Back to feeling like I don't know how to keep her alive, *bello*."

Dante dragged her even closer, and tucked her against his chest. There, she found safety, and home ... and love.

But where did Catherine find those things?

Nowhere, clearly.

11

The Attack

Dante POV

Dante paced.

Back and forth, back and forth.

Ten steps to the wall, and then ten steps back to the waiting room chair where he had been sitting. When nothing else could be done—when he could do nothing else—he paced.

The hospital waiting room was too quiet. A fucking echo of silence mocking him. A half a dozen pairs of eyes watched him.

A caged animal.

That's how he felt.

Wild.

Crazed.

Enraged.

His daughter—his *blood*—had damn near taken her own life. Downed two bottles of wine, and opened her wrist up like a flayed fish. She'd used a blade she popped out of a disposable razor.

Pink-stained water coming out from beneath the bathroom door had alerted him. His fears continued rising, and his calls to her went unheard. His fists beat hard against the door until bruises formed and his bones ached.

The memories were too fresh.

He suspected it would always feel that way.

Now, though, they only pissed him off.

The one question that seemed to be his constant companion since he had pulled his daughter from the bloodstained bathtub was ... *why?*

But the very second his mind posed the question, his black, bleeding heart already had an answer. One that was all too obvious. One that only served to enflame his growing rage even more.

Cross Donati.

How could this not be because of him? All the bad choices made and wrong roads traveled in Catherine's life seemed to lead straight back to that young man. Like a habit she couldn't kick, Catherine kept going back to Cross regardless of how badly she ended up hurt in the process.

Just two weeks earlier, something had happened again between the two. Not that Dante was entirely sure what had happened, but he knew something did. Catherine showed up on their doorstep with a bag in hand, tears in her eyes, and nothing else. She wouldn't talk when they pressed for details or reasons. She stayed shut away from them in her old room—avoiding.

The spiral downward had been obvious. She got worse and worse emotionally until ... tonight.

So, of course it was Cross.

It was always Cross.

That fucking—

"Son."

Dante spun on his heels to face his father. Antony's old eyes held nothing but sympathy and compassion. No pity—Antony Marcello pitied no one when he hated pity himself. Dante wished it helped on some level to soothe the rage festering inside as he looked at his father, but it really didn't. If anything, the rage festered up to his heart, and grew more. It only got wider, and bigger.

Why?

Because of every person in that waiting room. It was not just for Catherine's pain that had finally spilled over. It was not only for his wife's—and his own—pain. This pain had an echo. A reverberation of pain that continued on to each person it touched in their family.

All of them hurt for this.

So, he let that rage fester.

He wanted it to grow.

Nothing else felt right.

"You should sit," Antony told him. "Take a moment to rest while you can. I don't think you will find much time to do any of that in the coming days."

Dante shook his head. "No, I'm fine, Papa."

"You don't look fine."

"I am."

"Son—"

"Don't," Dante interjected quietly.

For once, he needed his father to let something go. He needed Antony to let him lie about this. To let him hide his feelings. He desperately needed his father not to push him right then.

Antony seemed to hear Dante's unspoken request. His father nodded once, and then clapped him on the shoulder.

"I'm going to take your mother home," Antony said. "She does need to rest whether she wants to admit it or not."

"No worries," Dante replied. "I'll give you a call when Catherine can have visitors or something. Or, if there's any updates."

"Thank you, son." Antony frowned. "And do try to rest, Dante. You do need it, too."

No, he needed violence.

Retribution.

Spilled blood …

He needed to get his rage out of his system, and only one person truly deserved it.

Still, he said, "Sure, Papa."

One more clap to Dante's shoulder, and his father was gone. Dante made sure to say a quick goodbye to his mother, too.

Catrina had fallen asleep on a chair while they waited for the final word that Catherine had been transferred upstairs. A place not meant for his daughter, except she needed it now.

Dante used his jacket to cover his wife, and brushed her stray red curls out of her face. For now, she slept peacefully, and without worry. He knew that would only last for as long as she kept her eyes closed, and stayed in dreamland. He hated that for his wife—hated knowing that she was feeling a kind of pain he could not help.

All over again, his rage swelled.

Only this time, there was no holding it back. There was no quelling it for a time until he could deal with it later.

It needed soothing *now*.

With one last look at his wife, Dante headed out of the waiting room. He was outside of the hospital, and halfway across the parking lot before someone finally caught up to him.

Lucian.

"Dante, wait."

He unlocked his Mercedes, and jumped in. Lucian slid into the passenger seat without a word. He didn't even look at his brother as they pulled out of the lot fast enough to make the tires squeal against the asphalt.

"I'm going to kill him," Dante finally said.

He didn't say who.

His brother didn't need him to.

Their families did not hide things from each other.

"You cannot kill Cross Donati, Dante."

"Can't and shouldn't are two very different things, Lucian."

"Won't, then. You *won't* kill him," Lucian said. "I'll make sure of it. For you, though, not for him."

"Put the gun away," Lucian said from behind Dante.

Dante knocked on the penthouse door again instead. Footsteps echoed from behind the wood.

"Dante, do not do something you will—"

Cross opened the penthouse door, and Dante had already cocked back his arm, and then let the gun smash into the man's face. Being pistol whipped was one thing—being beat with a gun like it was a man's fist was quite another.

Split lip.

Bruised face.

Cross on the floor.

That's what Dante wanted.

The sight of the blood already coming from Cross's mouth and nose was good, but not quite good enough. Cross's shouts echoed, but he didn't fight back.

Dante just kept going.

Another hit with the gun.

A kick to the ribs, and then another.

More fists.

More kicks.

"Fuck," Cross grunted, blood staining white teeth.

Cross tried to get away by turning to his side, and Dante reared back and kicked him in the face. Blood arched, and eyes rolled.

That might have been a bit much.

It still felt damn good to Dante.

"Dante, relax," Lucian growled.

"Fuck off, Lucian. You relax. Let it be your daughter, and you fucking relax."

"You can't kill—"

"I can do whatever the hell I want to, actually."

"You're not above retribution for this just because you are a boss," Lucian snarled.

Cross rolled to his back again, and Dante took great satisfaction in the sound of the man struggling to breathe. Blood spatters colored his lips. Bruises marred his face. He clutched at his ribs like they hurt, too.

Good.

Hurt like she does.

Dante leaned over Cross with his gun pointed at the man's face as Cross choked on blood.

He could only laugh.

The arrogant little shit could be knocked down.

Hard to believe.

"All right, Dante, you made your point," Lucian said. "Let's go."

Dante never looked away from Cross, and actually, grabbed his throat to keep him staring back. He had shit to say, and Cross needed to hear it.

He needed to fucking *heed* it.

"Stay the fuck away from my daughter from here on out," Dante said while his molars ached from clenching so hard. "Don't you ever even breathe in her direction again, Cross. Stay far the hell away. You come near me or mine again, and I will ruin you and yours. This city will crumble from what I will do to your family. In fact, make it easy on all of us and get the hell out of this state. Understood?"

Cross blinked.

Pain stared back at Dante.

It was not the same kind of pain Catherine had to be feeling, but it would do.

For now ...

"Understood?" Dante asked firmer.

"Yeah," Cross croaked.

Dante could have let him go with that said, but instead, he shifted his aim, and fired. The bullet tore through the top of Cross's shoulder. More blood spilled instantly. "So you'll have something to keep from this meeting. A reminder, if you will. A gift."

"Dante," Lucian hissed.

He stood, and left the penthouse, and Cross.

Let him fucking die there for all I care.

Lucian followed. "Now what, Dante? What will you do when his

father wants someone to answer for what you did tonight?"
   Dante said nothing.
   He now had nothing to say.

12

The Therapy

Catherine POV

It took four weeks, and eight sessions before Catherine opted to do something else other than greet Cara Guzzi from the floor. The therapist barely batted a lash at the sight of Catherine sitting on the bench in the window nook that overlooked the back property.

"Anything to see out there?" Cara asked.

The woman opted to stand rather than take a seat beside Catherine.

"Not at the moment," Catherine said. "All the snow should be gone by now, but it's not."

Cara gave Catherine one of her soft, warm smiles. "So, what exactly does it look like to you?"

Catherine looked out the window again, and took in the property. She chose to say the first things that came to her mind at the sight, and not filter her words like she might with someone else. Cara didn't like when Catherine filtered her thoughts and feelings.

"Cold and barren. There's no one out there, and none of the things that usually decorate our yard. The snow is far beyond the pretty point of winter—you know, when it's clean and bright, and sparkles somedays. Now, it's at that ugly stage where you can see everything it has killed as it made its way in. It's like the weather can't decide if it wants to be winter or spring right now."

"And so what does that do?"

"Well, it leaves you with a mess."

Cara laughed softly. "Or, you could be seeing something incredible at work here. Say ... a new start. A recharge, or a rebirth. The beginning stages of healing that a colder, lonelier time has left behind."

Catherine snuck a glance at Cara. She didn't think the woman was only talking about the snow and yard anymore. Cara did things like that quite often—delivered cryptic words meant to be advice. Catherine found herself spending days deciphering things Cara had told her.

On more than one occasion ...

"Did you try to do what we talked about during our last session?" Cara asked.

"I seriously considered it."

Cara openly frowned—something she didn't do very often. "But it sounds like perhaps you didn't actually follow through."

"No." Catherine looked toward the entryway. "Where are my parents today?"

"I believe your father said he was going to take your mother out for lunch. Don't worry, no one is listening in on our conversation, Catherine."

"No one ever does," Catherine replied. "You make sure of that."

Cara smiled. "I'm glad you trust me enough to believe that I will continue to keep that promise because I *will*."

Well, truthfully, at the moment, Cara was the only person Catherine trusted. She was the only person Catherine currently felt comfortable enough to have a conversation with that went deeper than the things on the surface of her life.

No one wanted to push Catherine.

Everyone was scared of hurting her.

The silence in her home was sometimes deafening. Not that she blamed her parents, or the rest of her family. What could they really do or say for her when they couldn't possibly understand her? It wasn't like she gave them anything to go on.

It was what it was.

"What stopped you from talking to Dante and Catrina?"

Catherine shrugged, and looked back at the window. Shoving her hands under her armpits, she wished in that moment that her oversized sweater would just swallow her whole.

Where she couldn't be seen ...

Where she didn't have to talk, or think ... or hurt.

Where she wasn't constantly being examined.

"I'm not ready to talk to them about my rape," Catherine finally said.

"But you have talked with me about it on several occasions," Cara pointed out.

"You're not them."

"Fair enough." Cara sighed, and then asked, "What do you think is the reason you're holding back—what is the issue keeping you at this not-ready stage, Catherine."

"I don't know."

"I think you do. Or you have a good idea of what it is. Otherwise, you would have no reason not to tell them, so they could help you and understand you more."

"But what if they don't?"

"Hmm?"

Catherine abused her bottom lip with her teeth until she could taste blood. Once she finally let her lip go, she clarified, "What if they don't understand at all—what if all they can do is find fault?"

"You think they'll blame you."

"I think that I don't want to find out."

"I genuinely believe that if you were honest with your parents, their response would probably surprise you."

Catherine scowled at her reflection in the window. Something she hadn't felt a lot lately came bubbling up before she even understood what was happening.

Irritation and anger.

The only thing she ever seemed to feel was lonely and empty.

It was strange.

And *good*.

"Why is it up to me?" she asked sharply.

Cara's calm demeanor didn't falter as Catherine turned on her. "What do you mean, Catherine?"

"Why is it always the victim who needs to tell—like it's our *only* fucking duty to report what happened to us? Why am I the one who's expected to relive my trauma again and again just to satisfy everyone else around me? I was raped—*me*. Not you, and not them. Just me. No one should ever have the right to demand a victim to do anything if they don't want to do it."

"It's not your trauma—it's only mine," Catherine finished.

She was a hell of a lot quieter at the end than she had started.

Funny how that worked.

For a long time, the women simply stared at one another. Cara said nothing, and Catherine waited the silence out.

She had said what she needed to say, after all.

Nothing more was needed.

"You're absolutely right," Cara finally said. "It's not my place to ask you to trigger yourself again and again by telling your story."

"Thank you."

"However …"

Catherine knew that *however* was coming. With Cara, there was always something else to be said or done.

"What?" Catherine asked.

"The longer you keep yourself in that mindset—the one of a victim—the harder it will be to leave it behind. Many women who have been assaulted don't like to think of themselves as victims, but survivors. See, they have come out on the other side of their attack, handled the trauma it caused, and walked through the destruction it left behind."

Cara smiled, adding, "In other words, Catherine, they *survived*. A victim is still processing, and not yet beyond that mindset."

"So, maybe that's what I need to be right now," Catherine replied, shrugging. "A victim. Maybe I'm not ready to move beyond something I have barely allowed myself to think about, not to mention, considering telling someone else."

"Maybe," Cara agreed. "Or, maybe this place is comfortable and familiar to you. This place is easier to control how it leaves you feeling. It probably allows you to control how close you allow others, too."

Catherine didn't like how a lot of what Cara said made a hell of a lot of sense. She wasn't ready to do anything.

"Maybe I don't want them to see me as a victim, too," Catherine mumbled.

Cara nodded. "I can understand that."

"You don't agree, though."

"Catherine, this is your journey, not mine. I may push or encourage you in certain directions, but ultimately, it will always be you who chooses which road you want to travel."

"Oh."

"Yes," Cara said quietly. "Now, I was thinking … why don't we take a drive today? Go somewhere—do something new for this session."

Catherine's heart thumped hard in her throat at the prospect of getting out of the house without one of her parents practically holding her hand like a child. "Seriously?"

Cara pulled out a set of familiar keys. They belonged to Catherine's matte black Lexus. Her father kept them well hidden.

"Where did you get those?" Catherine asked. "My dad took them away months ago."

"I explained to him why he needed to give them back."

"And why was that?"

"Because you are an adult, and not his child to punish. While I know he didn't take the keys to punish you, I bet it still felt like it. Right?"

"Kind of."

"Exactly. That certainly won't breed anything good between the two of you. Contempt, maybe. He couldn't hand over the keys fast enough at that point."

Catherine swallowed hard. "Huh."

Cara jingled the keys. "Wherever you want to go, Catherine, we will go today."

She grabbed the keys faster than she thought was possible.

"The beach. I want to go to the beach."

13

The Separation

Cross POV

This is what hell must feel like.
Cross's inner thoughts were like a constant form of torture lately that just wouldn't let him go. It didn't seem to matter what he was doing, or where he was, his mind and tar-black heart managed to somehow drag him even lower.

Emotionally, that was.

So was his life now.

The filled-to-capacity Chicago nightclub was supposed to be the hottest place in the city. At least, that's what everybody said when Cross asked. It certainly had enough people partying inside to say it was popular.

A good place to escape.

Somewhere life couldn't touch them.

Just what Cross thought he needed.

Yet, there he sat in a back booth, a full glass of whiskey untouched in front of him, and entirely stuck inside his own head and heart. Not even the conversation between his two friends could drive him out of his thoughts enough to engage them. The great music and beautiful, dancing women with dresses short enough to show off peeks of their ass cheeks did nothing for him, either.

Six months in Chicago—six months without Catherine—and one might think Cross would have finally left New York, and her, behind.

Life was not so simple.

His heart was also a fickle bitch.

"Yo, Cross."

He blinked out of his depressing thoughts, and looked at his friend. Zeke sat beside him in the booth, while Tommaso sat alone on the other side. Both guys looked at him like he had grown a second head or something.

"What?" Cross asked.

"Man, you're out of it tonight, huh?" Zeke asked.

"He's like this a lot, really," Tommaso said.

Cross gave the youngest of the three a look of warning. "I don't remember anyone asking you, Tom."

"Still said it."

"Be careful, Tom," Cross said, smirking, "or I might let one of the bouncers know your ID is a fake."

"Mob-owned joint," Tommaso countered. "Not worried about it."

Cross figured.

He turned to Zeke instead, saying, "It's just been a long day, man."

"Sure," Zeke replied.

Zeke didn't sound like he really believed it, though. Honestly, Cross hadn't been making much of an effort to hide his shitty moods, either. His troubles were on his sleeve for everybody to see, lately.

"It's your first night in the city," Cross told Zeke, "so don't be worrying about me, man."

Zeke scoffed. "First, how can I even look out for you if you won't talk to me about shit, huh? As for the second thing—I've got a couple of weeks to bug the shit out of you if you want to do this the hard way, Cross. Better to get it over with now."

Cross chuckled. "You're a fucker."

"Kind of have to be when my best friend is living a couple of states away from me, now."

"I like him," Tommaso said, tipping his glass in Zeke's direction.

Cross ignored Tommaso, and looked at Zeke again. "I'm fine."

"Are you?"

He didn't—nor was he interested in—getting the first degree from his friends. Besides, he didn't talk *feelings*. He just wasn't the type.

It wasn't his style.

Not giving Zeke a chance to question him further, Cross pushed out of the booth. "I've got to go take a piss."

Neither of the guys moved to follow Cross. Men weren't like women who always seemed to need to use the bathroom in groups.

Like a fucking book club for bathrooms.

Not bothering to chat more with his friends before he left, Cross weaved in and out of the dancing people on the main floor of the club. The place was so full that it was starting to feel a little claustrophobic.

Suffocating, even.

Soon, Cross was closed in the men's bathroom. He relieved himself at the furthest urinal from the drunk trying to figure out where his piss was supposed to go.

A fucking shame, really.

Men like him—criminals—were labeled stains on society, but there was that stupid drunk. Shitfaced, and fucking stumbling around like a fool. At least men like him didn't get smashed and make public scenes of themselves.

They did have standards.

Cross zipped up, and headed for the sinks. He took a little bit longer to wash his hands, but that was simply because he wasn't ready to head back to the table just yet. Zeke would have more questions. He would push and prod until he got something from Cross that satisfied him. It was just how the two were in their friendship.

This time, he wished that Zeke wouldn't do that at all.

He didn't want to talk.

Not about what sent him to Chicago.

Not about New York.

Not about *Catherine*.

None of it.

Cross stared at his reflection in the mirror.

The bruises from Dante's beating were finally gone—it had only taken a couple of weeks for those to yellow, and heal. He needed a fucking haircut, but the barber he preferred was in New York, and he didn't trust anybody yet in Chicago to do it.

He kind of depended on Zeke to look out for Camilla while Cross wasn't close enough to do it. He missed his mother's cooking on Sunday afternoons like nothing else. He wished the calls he made to Calisto were enough to satisfy his need to have his step-father close, but they weren't even close.

Nothing was good enough.

Chicago wasn't New York.

The people here could never replace the people there.

Mostly, he missed Catherine.

Cross met his own gaze in the mirror. All over again, he was stuck reminding himself that this was for the best.

For her.

Even if it fucking killed him ...
She's better off.
She needs to get better.
She can't do that with you.
It was his mantra on repeat.

Cross headed out of the bathroom, and unsurprisingly, found Zeke waiting for him. His friend leaned against the wall across from the bathroom. Cross joined him.

"I'm fine," he said again.

Zeke nodded. "I know you're not."

"Yeah, well ..."

"Yeah," Zeke echoed.

A girl with a pretty face walked past them, and eyed Cross the whole way. She didn't even attempt to hide her interest in the slightest.

"Maybe something like that is what you need," Zeke murmured, eyeing the girl's backside. "If you don't want to talk your shit out, then why not try fucking it out with somebody?"

"Maybe," Cross replied.

He headed in the opposite direction than the woman had gone.

"But no thanks," he added.

14

The Aftermath

Catrina POV

With Cross Donati gone from the private dining area, the space turned deathly silent. Such an abnormal thing for these men surrounding Catrina. They very rarely found themselves rendered speechless.

She supposed an attack like the one Cross launched upon her husband would do just that—leave them all without the right words to say.

Sometimes, Catrina thought—as much as she loved him—that Dante could be a bit too complacent. Too comfortable, so to speak, in his position at the top. He rarely came up against someone who did not fear him in some way.

Catrina knew the truth the second Cross left without looking back.

Her husband learned then, too ...

Cross Donati did not fear Dante Marcello.

Catrina didn't have the first clue if that made things worse, or not. She really didn't have the time to figure it out, all things considered.

"Boss, I didn't mean for him to get past me like that," the enforcer said. "He just—"

"Shut the fuck up," Dante snarled.

"I—"

"Get out!"

Her husband's roar could have shattered glass from the volume. His face reddened, his teeth clenched, and he balled his fists tightly at his sides. The calm demeanor Dante usually sported was officially lost. His appearance—much like hers—was of the utmost importance to them. Nothing should shake it.

He had lost that hold on his control. She worried, but silently.

"Did I fucking stutter?" Dante shouted at his balking enforcer. "I said get out!"

The man didn't need to be told again. He hightailed it from the private space without a look back. The whole time, Dante glared at the empty space the enforcer left behind.

"I want him appropriately punished for that error," Dante hissed at Lucian.

"It could have happened to any man holding the door," Lucian countered. "He's a good enforcer, Dante. Don't create unneeded tension."

"If he's such a good enforcer, then he will be a far better one after he is taught a lesson for what happened here today."

Lucian opened his mouth again—likely to protest his brother's demand even more. He quickly snapped his mouth shut when Dante's burning glare turned on him.

Dante's gaze screamed silent threats. A curl of his lips promised fast violence. His posture showed his position without him even needing to actually say a damn thing.

Normally, Catrina would appreciate those things about her husband. Right then, however, they all concerned her.

"I'll have something done," Lucian muttered.

"Make sure of it."

Catrina replaced her knife to the sheath at her inner thigh. Beneath the skirt of her dress, the weapon couldn't be seen. Despite her husband's protests over the years, she still preferred a sharp, small knife to a loud, clunky gun.

For obvious reasons ...

Like today.

Cross had not flinched when the guns came out to play. Catrina and her knife, however, had certainly made him hesitate, and swallow a little harder. For only a moment, sure, but a moment was all she needed from a man to end him.

"As for that fucking Donati bastard," Dante said, still looking at his brother, "I want something done with him, too. *Soon.*"

"No."

"You will do what I tell you to do, Lucian."

"Not in this case. I will not."

Catrina's gaze jumped between her husband, and his brother. They rarely fought, and she was unsure if she wanted to step in the middle of this particular battle. She tried to stay out of Dante's business, much like he stayed out of hers. It was the respect of the matter, and it allowed them both to work without added complications.

This, though, was not quite the same.

It was beyond business.

It was family, too.

Their *daughter*.

She understood Dante's position.

Lucian's, on the other hand, could also not be ignored.

Not after the things Cross had said.

"I stand where I said with Cross," Lucian said, "and nothing you say or order will move me on it. After everything you did to him back then, he was owed this moment. Maybe he waited longer than I would have to get retribution, but that was his choice to make. It could have been far worse than what you got today, Dante, and you know it."

"You—"

"What will you do?" Lucian asked, not even giving his brother a chance to speak. "Will you punish me for being disobedient? I dare you to try, brother."

The two men quieted—both silently seething between their stiffened postures, and hard glares. Catrina finally decided then that she had enough. This was all more than she could handle at the moment.

With a subtle nod at Lucian to gain his attention, she pointed a single red-tipped fingernail at the doorway. "Leave, Lucian."

"Catrina," Dante said, stepping in, "we are not done talking."

"I can assure you that you are done, *bello*."

"I'll be around," Lucian said.

That was that.

He was gone the next second.

Dante turned on Catrina as soon as Lucian was out of sight. "What in the hell do you think you're doing stepping in on my business like that, Catrina?"

She bristled at his tone, but hid it well. Carefully brushing down her dress, and then fixing her curls, Catrina said nothing while Dante continued ranting on. She would give him a minute or two.

He was warranted that, sure.

Not much more.

After all, she now had things to say, too.

"Don't you ever do something like that to me again," she heard him say.

Catrina turned a cold smile on her husband. "Or what, Dante?"

His gaze blazed.

Her coldness remained.

"Fix yourself," Catrina hissed at him darkly. "Look at you, Dante. Acting like a stupid fool in a public restaurant. Why not just pull your gun out and wave it around, too? Really make a scene for us, if that's what you're trying to do. Marcellos don't half-ass anything, after all."

"I beg your fucking pardon?"

Catrina didn't back down. "Fix the mess you are making of yourself, *bello*, or we will not be leaving here together."

It would not be a very pleasant day in their marriage, never mind once they were actually home. She knew it already.

Still, Catrina held her ground. Sometimes, she had come to learn with her husband, this was exactly the kind of thing he needed her to do. Besides, had he wanted an easier, more compliant woman, he would not have married her.

Dante took a deep breath, and schooled his features. Still, his eyes blazed and his fists clenched. That rage of his would not be going away for a while. It was not something Catrina would be able to soothe for him.

"Was that why I woke up alone in the ER the night of Catherine's suicide attempt?" Catrina asked. "Because you had left to go after Cross?"

The look he passed her said it all.

She still needed to hear him say it.

"Dante, you *will* tell me."

"Yes," he growled.

Catrina nodded, and let out a sound that voiced her disgust. "Why, because you blamed him?"

"Obviously."

"Use that attitude with me again, Dante."

Dante checked himself. "My apologies."

Catrina wished it helped.

She knew it wouldn't.

Certainly not for their daughter, anyway.

"You had better work on something far better than an apology to fix this, Dante. Start now."

15

The Day

Cross POV

The reflection in the tall, stand-up mirror was a familiar sight, and yet, somehow new, too. It certainly wasn't the first time that Cross had seen himself in a tux. He'd worn a bowtie before.

And yet, none of this was the same at all.

It was his wedding day, after all. His one and only wedding day. There would never be another day like this one in his lifetime.

Not when he was marrying his childhood love. Catherine had always been the girl of his fucking dreams.

Cross intended to soak in every moment of this day that he possibly could. He couldn't wait to marry Catherine, but he also didn't want to rush the day, either. Not if that meant he might miss something.

He had been waiting for this day for far longer than he could even remember. It was finally time to enjoy what this day actually meant.

Always.

It meant *always*.

Cross tugged up the sleeve of his jacket, and checked his watch. A new gold Rolex with diamonds on the tips of the minute and second hands. A gift—for his wedding—from his sister and her husband.

They knew his tastes well.

The time said he only had a short while left before he needed to go downstairs, and take his spot. The knock on the door of the private room drew Cross's attention away from the time and his reflection in the mirror.

"Yeah, it's open," Cross said.

His mother and father slipped into the room, and quickly closed the door behind them. He still heard the murmurings of those who were gathered outside waiting for him to finally come out. Their family and friends, and probably some of Catherine's people, too.

His mother gave him a brilliant smile, while his father whistled low.

"Look at you," Calisto said.

Cross chuckled. "You say that like I don't look good every day, or something."

His father grinned. "You and that arrogance, son."

"Wouldn't be me without it."

Emma's laughter colored up the room. "No, it definitely would not be you, my boy."

Calisto stepped aside to let his wife come closer to their son. Emma's outstretched—warm and familiar—hands cupped Cross's cheeks. Her hands that had never hurt him, and only showered him with love throughout his life.

He adored his mother.

"How did the dress reveal go at the Astoria?" she asked.

"Amazing."

Emma beamed. "Yes?"

"Yeah, Ma." Cross shrugged. "She's so beautiful. Blew my damn mind."

"Really?"

Cross laughed. "I might have cried a little."

Emma stroked his smiling cheeks with her thumbs, and her gaze glistened with unshed tears. "I hope you know that we're all so happy for you. We are all so proud of you, Cross."

"Yeah, I know."

"And you do look quite handsome."

Cross pulled his mother closer, and kissed Emma's forehead. He felt her soften at the action, and her fingertips patted his cheeks. Their silent *I love yous*.

"How ready are you for this day?" his mother asked.

"Beyond ready."

"That's the only answer I want to hear." Emma let him go, and reached for her clutch Calisto held. "I have something for you—for good luck."

"You didn't need to get me anything."

Emma waved a hand high. "It's a silly little thing, really."

"Well, thanks, Emmy," Calisto grumbled.

She looked back at her husband, but just as quickly, her gaze came back to Cross. "A silly little thing that means the absolute world to me. Call it my good luck charm, I guess."

His mother pulled out a small poker chip from the clutch, and handed it over. Cross eyed the chip, and ran his fingertip across the embossed letters on top. Then, he squeezed it tight in his palm to keep it safe.

He didn't need details about it, where it came from, or why his mother wanted him to have it. Just the fact that she had given it to him—and on his wedding day, no less—was more than enough for him to cherish it.

It had been hers.

That alone made it special.

"Thanks, Ma."

Emma patted his cheek once more. "Our wild child—I always knew you were going to be amazing, Cross. I love you."

"I love you, too."

Emma gave him one more smile and kiss, said her goodbye, and then left him alone in the room with his father. Calisto came close enough to slap Cross on the shoulder, and waved at the two chairs resting beneath a large painting.

"Sit with me?" Calisto asked.

Cross did, and the two stayed quiet like that for a few moments. He didn't mind the silence. Not when it came to his father. Some of his most fondest memories with Calisto were moments just like this one.

Finally, Cross said, "Thank you, Papa."

Calisto glanced over at him. "For what, my boy?"

"A lot of things."

"Try me."

"Being mine—my father. For doing the wrong thing with Ma all those years ago when doing the right thing probably would have been a hell of a lot easier. For making me who I am, and for loving me despite of it. Thank you."

Calisto simply stared at Cross for a long while, saying nothing. He didn't mind that, either. He had needed to say those things—to make sure his father knew what was inside his heart because he didn't often express it well otherwise.

"You are everything that I ever did right, Cross," Calisto said, "even when it was wrong."

"Yeah, I know that, now."

"I'm glad this cycle of lies in our family and in our bloodline ends with you. I was never very proud to carry this name—Donati. It only reminded me of pain."

"And now?"

Calisto smiled. "Well, now …"

"Hmm?"

"Now, it reminds me of us—of your mother, of you and of your sister. You all have given me every reason to be proud of our name, and not ashamed. And today, we get to add another Donati to the mix."

Yes.

Catherine, that was.

Catherine Donati.

16

The Night

Cross POV

The bouquet flew high, and Cross was already closing the distance between him and his new bride before anyone even caught the flowers. Catherine—in her blush-colored wedding gown fit for a queen—saw him coming her way.

She tossed back her head with a laugh. A few—or a couple of hundred—of their guests saw him cutting across the dance floor, and they laughed, too.

He had warned Catherine, after all. Hell, he warned anybody who dared to listen to him throughout their very large, and very *long*, reception.

Once she tossed those flowers, it was done.

They were out of there.

The first dance was long over, just like the four course meal, and cake cutting. He had held back from smearing cake in Catherine's face after she painted his with icing, but only barely. She looked far too beautiful to be doing that, anyway.

He had made sure to give their guests a bit of a show when he had to collect Catherine's garter, and toss it into a waiting crowd of single men.

Yes, they had certainly made sure their guests were properly entertained, fed, and satisfied. The Donati and Marcello union had been—by far—one of the biggest events in the city over the last decade. No expense was spared, and they had not disappointed.

But now it was over.

And Cross was done.

Cross caught Catherine around the waist with one arm. In one swift, easy pull, he had her lifted from the floor, and tossed over his shoulder. Cheers, hollers, and whoops echoed out from behind them as Cross headed for the front entrance of the Waldorf Astoria hotel.

The crinoline of Catherine's dress flew all around them as she kicked her legs. Her laughter was a teasing, breathless whisper in his ear. She smacked his back with her palm.

"What do you think you are doing?" she asked.

"Getting us out of here. It's the only way I can, apparently."

People kept dragging her away all night.

"I can walk, you know!"

"Cool fact."

Catherine laughed again. "You have to let us say goodbye, Cross."

"Babe, we have been saying goodbye all damn night. We are leaving. *Now.*"

People rushed ahead of them. Some were still shouting, cheering, and going on in their way. They filled up the entrance, and flooded out the doors onto the front steps. Of course, they left a clean walkway for Cross to walk straight through.

Outside, his and Catherine's families waited. Only then did he hoist her off his shoulder, and set her to the ground.

"Have a good trip," Dante told Catherine. Then, the man looked at Cross. "And you …"

"Hmm?"

Dante smiled. "You lasted longer in there than I thought you would."

Cross laughed, and took the hand that Dante offered. The two shook hands, before Dante clapped him on the shoulder.

Shit wasn't perfect with them.

It was going to take time.

Cross was willing to make time, though.

Catherine was currently distracted by her mother, and brother. Even his mother and father were in the group saying goodbye to his wife.

Cross turned back to Dante. "Thank you."

"For?"

"Her."

Dante nodded. "Of course."

"Someone is impatient," Zeke said.

Cross laughed when he glanced over his shoulder. Catherine was already climbing the stairs leading to the private jet. She hadn't even wanted to make a stop to get out of her wedding dress. The gown billowed around her legs in all directions from the wind. From the top of the stairs, she waved at him.

A silent, *hurry the fuck up, Cross*.

After all, it had been him who dragged her out of their reception because he simply couldn't wait any longer.

Cross winked, and waved right back.

Catherine only shook her head, and then proceeded to enter the plane. She could wait five more minutes, surely.

"Yeah, well, this has been a long time coming," Cross finally said to his friend.

Zeke nodded. "Have a good honeymoon."

Cross grinned. "You know it."

"I'll hold the city down for you."

"You better."

Zeke held out his fist, and Cross bumped it with his own.

Ride or die.

"And I guess, thanks for being my best man," Cross said. "From the start, huh?"

Zeke chuckled. "Sometimes I swear that's all I know how to do."

"It's not a bad thing."

"Never said it was." Zeke gestured over Cross's shoulder. "Someone's back out, and looking this way."

Sure enough, Catherine was standing back out on the stairs again.

"Call me when you get five minutes," Zeke said.

"Not likely."

Zeke shrugged. "Yeah, I wouldn't call your ass, either."

The two friends hugged fast, and then let each other go. Soon, Cross was climbing the stairs of the private jet, and heading inside. They still had another hour to go before the plane would be able to lift off, but he didn't mind.

The pilot and flight attendant greeted him at the front of the plane.

"Your wife is changing in the bedroom at the back," the blonde flight attendant said.

The pilot chuckled. "If you would like, we can let you both know when you need to take your seats."

"That'd be great, thanks."

The two of them nodded, and then disappeared into the cockpit. Cross headed down the middle aisle, and was at the back of the plane in less than a minute. He found the door was closed, but a single knock granted him entrance.

Cross barely got the door closed before Catherine was on him. Her kiss slammed against his mouth, and seared him into nothing but ashes from the inside out. His hands found soft skin—she'd apparently gotten that dress off all by herself, but he had no idea how.

"Let's just get these off," his wife said.

Her quick hands had his pants undone, and shoved down in a couple of seconds, and a single breath. Her fingers circled his length, and stroked him hard with tight palms. He hardened under her touch in no time at all.

"Jesus Christ," he grunted.

Catherine's sly grin clouded his vision before she was gone. Dropping to her knees, he'd barely blinked before her mouth found his cock. She took every inch of him between those silken lips, sucked him all the way back to her throat, and practically grabbed the fucking air right out of his chest.

Her tongue swirled, stroked, and teased. Those teeth of hers dragged gently enough to make his nerves snap.

Jesus.

Fuck him if he didn't love the way Catherine sucked him off. He adored the way she looked on her knees, taking his cock like it was her favorite thing to do. Those green eyes of hers watering every time she took just a little too much of him in.

But hell, if that was the game she wanted to play …

Cross let Catherine tease him for a short while, but soon, he was wanting something else a hell of a lot more. Yanking her up from floor, he spun his already naked wife around, and bent her over the bed.

Shit.

He reminded himself to thank Zeke and Wolf for the gift of the private jet. Particularly, a jet with a bed and room.

Catherine's laughter came out breathless and spun as Cross's hands dragged up her spine. He tugged the silk tie from around his neck, and used it to bind her hands at her back. Over her shoulder, Catherine tossed him one of her sweet winks, and then another sly grin.

"Maybe we should wait a bit," she told him. "Another, what, hour? Yeah, an hour and we'll be up in the air. Join the mile high club and all that."

Cross didn't fucking think so.

"Oh, don't worry," he said, "we'll have another go."

But for now ...

He fitted himself behind Catherine, slid the head of his cock through her slick folds, and took her in one thrust. The force put her up on her toes, and she let out a satisfied hiss.

The sound rocked him.

Pleased him.

Drove him fucking crazy.

He pulled out, and slammed right back inside of her pussy again just to hear her make that sound one more time. She did, and her fingernails dragged red lines across his hands. He was still holding onto the hands he had tied at her back, after all.

Cross didn't even mind the marks.

He loved the sting.

It felt kind of appropriate, really.

This woman had left marks all over him.

All throughout their life.

Their love kind of stung, too.

Damn good.

"Come on, then," Catherine urged, "make me come."

Cross only really needed her to ask, and his baser urges came out to play. It was damn near as tempting as the sound of her begging.

Still just as good, though.

And then she did just that.

Whispered, "*Please.*"

He was done for.

His control was gone.

Cross found that fucking Catherine now that they were married wasn't any different than before they said their vows, but somehow, it still felt new.

All his.

She was all his, now.

He had just finished wiping his cum from his wife's back with his silk pocket square when the flight attendant knocked on the door.

Catherine sighed, and gave Cross a look.

"What?" he asked.

"I was going to save that—put it in our shadow box, or something."

Ah, well ...

Shit.

He looked at the ruined item. "I could have it dry—"

Catherine yanked it out of his hand. "*No*, Cross."

"It was a thought."

"Here's a thought—you had three groomsmen, and a best man. Make sure one of them keeps theirs."

He could do that.

Happy wife, happy life.

17

The Daughter

Cross POV

"You okay?"

Cross looked up from the sound of his father-in-law's voice to find Dante had finally arrived at their house. How long had Cross been leaning against the wall in some kind of awful fucking daze he just couldn't shake?

Hours.

It had to be *hours*.

Cross blinked. "Yeah, I'm just—"

"Tired," Dante said. "This is a long fucking process, I know."

Nodding, Cross straightened up, and felt his spine crack. *Jesus.* That kind of hurt, but it felt good at the same time. How was that even fucking possible?

What a day.

A beautiful day.

But still ...

"Go grab a quick nap," Dante told him, tipping his head to the side as if to encourage Cross to move. "In the spare bedroom, or something. Cat is downstairs getting some food warmed up that she brought over, so I don't think Catherine will even notice you're gone."

Cross frowned. "I don't think I should. That wouldn't be very fair to her, would it?"

Dante cocked a brow. "Listen, *you* need to sleep, too. Because when that little girl is here, Catherine's not going to be. This is exhausting—she's running on adrenaline right now. But once the baby gets here, all that adrenaline goes away, and her mind needs to recharge. Who do you think is going to be left with the task of taking care of the baby?"

"Oh."

"Yeah, oh. Go—I'll cover for you, anyway."

Cross grinned at the way his father-in-law almost sounded ... conspiratorial about Cross taking a fucking nap while Catherine had to labor through the early contractions. She had been laboring for eight hours now—all goddamn night. The birthing classes they took to prepare for this day had told them this portion could take hours, or even a day or two, before it would move onto the next phase when they would recommend she come into the hospital.

Catherine was fine with that.

Then, she was going to demand an epidural.

Her plan was *clear*.

Cross saw no issue there.

None at all.

"Don't make me tell you again," Dante said, jerking his thumb to the side, "this is going to take a while, Cross."

"All right."

He could hear the running shower that Catherine had been using as a stress reliever for the last *hour* even as he slipped into the spare bedroom down the hall from their master bedroom. He didn't know how long their hot water tank would hold up considering when he went into the bathroom, it seemed like she had it turned up to just below scalding.

But whatever made her happy.

Jesus, right now, that was all he cared about.

Soon, his little girl would be here.

His *principessa*.

Perfect little Cece Catherine.

The next Donati girl.

Cross's head hit the pillow on the spare bed, and he was positive he fell asleep before his eyes even closed fully.

He still felt bad.

He should have stayed up.

His body was done.

Cross woke up to the sound of beeping. A familiar beep that made him want to curse, and ignore it altogether. It only took him one second of being awake for panic to settle into his chest, and remind him why he shouldn't be fucking sleeping in the first place.

Catherine.

Labor.

Shit.

Cross jumped up from the bed, and grabbed his cell phone at the same time—the offending device being the thing that was making all that beeping noise. He checked the screen as he headed out of the spare bedroom.

Any updates?

His father.

Another text he missed from Zeke.

Is my Goddaughter here yet, or what?

Damn.

How long had he been sleeping, anyway?

Cross checked the time on the phone as he took the stairs of their Newport home two at a time. He blinked at the time staring back at him.

He'd only slept a little more than an hour.

It felt like *way* more.

Well, maybe he shouldn't complain, then.

Cross quickly typed replies back to his father, and Zeke. No news yet to tell, and he would let them know when something changed, but not to hold their breaths.

His foot hit the downstairs hardwood floor, and he hesitated at the sound of laughter coming from the kitchen area. And also, *music.*

What in the fuc—

"Come on, now," he heard Catrina say, "don't give me that look Catherine. I swear this is what your father did for me—worked like a charm, baby."

"It did," Dante agreed.

"You really think I want to dance right now, Ma?" Catherine asked, laughing.

"Dancing moves the baby down. Dancing helps. Dancing makes you *happy.*"

"So dance," Dante added.

Cross quietly moved down the hall, and poked his head around the kitchen entryway. Sure enough, his very pregnant wife was being slowly cajoled into dancing to a very fast, modern song that he recognized from the radio.

Oh, she loved music.

Loved to dance.

He leaned against the entryway, and watched as a beautiful, wide smile bloomed over Catherine's features as she took her mother's hands in her own, and began to dance. A quick beat that had her feet moving, and her hips swaying.

God.

She was so beautiful.

More so now that she was pregnant with his child, and so full of life. It was amazing how something like this could change a man.

Their whole life had been like that, though. *They* had always been like that.

Amazing.

Breathtaking.

Crazy.

Perfect.

Across the room at the table, Dante looked Cross's way, and gave him a nod. Cross returned it silently. Catherine and Catrina didn't notice him standing there.

And then …

"*Oh*, shit," Catherine breathed.

Her dancing stopped.

He recognized that pained look in her eye just before she grabbed the counter with one hand, and her mother's wrist with the other. Catrina was down on one knee before her daughter—Cross was pretty sure this was the first time he had ever seen his mother-in-law dressed down with no makeup, and no high heels on.

"Breathe," Catrina murmured.

"I am," Catherine whined.

The contractions were clearly stronger.

She'd been fine to walk through them earlier.

Maybe dancing did help.

"I just want … where is—"

He knew what she was going to say before she did it. He crossed the room before she could get the words out.

"Right here, babe," Cross said.

Catherine let go of the counter, and grabbed hold of Cross instead.

"Could I …?"

Dante's hands reached for the swaddled bundle of pink that Cross had finally brought out to show their waiting family. He held a little tighter to his daughter—entirely unwilling to let her go just yet.

Little Cece slept peacefully. All cleaned now from birth, and happy as could be. Her puffy cheeks puffed out even more as she sucked on the side of her hand that had somehow broken free of the swaddle.

She had dark eyes like his, though they were closed right now. Dark hair like his, too. But those bow-shaped lips, the shape of her face, and more …

That was all her mother.

And she was perfect.

Oh, so perfect.

"I just, uh …"

"Not quite ready to let her go, son," Calisto said, chuckling.

Emma grinned beside her husband. "Calisto was the same way with Cam."

"And Dante, with Catherine," Catrina added.

Dante gave his wife a look. "I was not."

"Really, so you didn't refuse to allow your brothers to hold Catherine when they came to visit. Oh, and your mother, too. Except your father snapped at you, and then you let her hold Catty. I swear, it was cute—"

"That's enough of that," Dante grumbled.

Laughter lit up the family waiting room.

Zeke came a little closer, and peered over Cross's shoulder. "Look at her, man."

"I know," Cross murmured.

"She looks like her mother."

"I know."

And good God, that in itself was amazing and scary enough. He was holding his whole life in his hands. Every good part of his heart and soul was in this child.

He was not a good man.

He was criminal.

He lived in the gray.

What did he do to deserve the perfection he was holding?

What angel was looking out for him?

Cece made a face, and then those eyelashes of hers started to flutter a bit. Eyelashes for days, really. Her eyes opened, and she locked gazes with her father.

The world stopped turning for a second.

It was like she *knew*.

He could feel it.

She knew who he was.

The birthing classes had told them that newborns couldn't see very well for a while after being born. That their vision needed time to adjust, and most things were cloudy to them.

Cross didn't know about that. His daughter looked at him like she had been waiting to find her daddy for a long time.

"Hey, *principessa*," he murmured. "Look at you, *mia bambina*. You're so perfect."

He teased her little clenched fist with his fingertip, and quickly, she wrapped her whole hand instinctively around his finger. She held tight, even minutes later when Cross handed her off to Dante for the first time.

His mother said he had to.

Still, Cece kept hold of his finger.

"Someone knows who their daddy is," Dante murmured, gazing between his granddaughter, and Cross. "My God, she looks like her mother."

"Déjà vu?" Catrina asked.

Dante nodded. "Yeah, Cat. Just like déjà vu."

He didn't know what the two were talking about, but the silent look they shared told him not to ask.

Somethings were private.

They were meant to stay that way.

Uruly Era Shorts

18

The Trainees

Cross POV

Andino Marcello was fucking with Cross. He had to be. How else would the Marcello boss explain the utter fucking bullshit Cross was having to deal with right now?

Bullshit was being kind, really.

Cross was now—with no affection in his delivery—referring to the idiots that Andino had sent to him as simply The Fucks. One Fuck, Two Fuck, Three Fuck, Four Fuck, Five Fuck, and Six Fuck.

Six entirely useless fucks who Cross was supposed to train for Andino to apparently run guns for his operation. If there was ever a reason for a woman to swallow a load—it was those foolish idiots Andino sent to him.

The world would not have been a lonelier place without their lives added to the mix, as far as Cross was concerned.

Jesus.

Send me your best guys, Cross had told Andino. He was then, in turn, supposed to make the guys into the best weapons runners that Andino had ever seen. With these fucks, that was going to be entirely impossible. They were so useless to Cross, in fact, that he couldn't even be bothered to learn their names.

Hence, The Fucks.

It was the best he could do.

Insubordinate.

Ignorant.

Arrogant.

Downright stupid at times.

They couldn't follow direction, had zero understanding of how to shut up and listen, and Cross was seriously concerned about safety when it came to these idiots having guns in their hands.

They were not gunrunning material.

None of them.

Cross knew it from the moment they walked into the warehouse on day one. They were a bunch of boys playing pretend—idiots dressing up as even bigger fools. No one with any sense would think this was a good idea to use them as gunrunners.

Fuck One had no idea how to properly load a mag. Fuck Two was so lazy that Cross had caught the guy taking a nap in the corner—for the *second* time. Fuck Three left his phone where Cross could see it, and thus, also the texted pictures of guns the guy had sent to his girlfriend.

And that was just three of them.

The other three?

Just as bad.

If not worse.

Cross tried—fuck knows he tried to do something with these guys. Something to turn them into useable, moldable men. Even … possibly … potential made men for Andino, and not just gunrunners.

It was impossible.

The Lord was testing him.

That's what it had to be.

God was having a good moment.

A joke at Cross's expense.

A loud clang followed by the unmistakable pop going off broke Cross from his daze. A break he had taken away from those idiots to try and at least relax for five goddamn minutes, so he didn't kill one of them.

A shout echoed.

Then, a curse.

"Oh, my fucking God," one of the guys mumbled loudly.

"What now?" Cross groaned.

Because apparently, he couldn't even have those five fucking minutes to himself. He should have known better, frankly. Like damn children, these fools couldn't be left to their own devices. They had to constantly watched—babysat like *babies*.

"Boss, boss!"

Cross pushed away from the office wall, and headed for the door with a sigh. No, even calling them children was too nice, honestly. His two kids were far better behaved than these fucks, and Naz was still just a newborn, for Christ's sake.

"What the hell do you guys need now?" Cross asked as he came out onto the warehouse's main floor. "What are you all standing there for?"

Five of the fucks stood in a semi-circle facing Cross.

He noticed a problem instantly.

"Where's the other fuc—guy?"

Fuck One—the idiot with the issues learning how to load bullets and handle a gun was standing in the middle with a semi-automatic hanging from his limp hand. He looked as though he had seen a ghost.

White all over.

"What happened?" Cross boomed.

Maybe if he spoke louder, they would listen better.

Doubtful.

The five men—all with wide eyes—moved slightly further away from the fuck with the gun. None of them particularly looked like they trusted the guy all that much at the moment. Which was strange because one thing the six idiots did have was comradery between them. That would have been great if they all had even an ounce of common sense to add in with it, though.

Something they *didn't* have.

At all.

Cross came closer.

Finally, he saw what they had been standing in front of. Or rather, what they all had been trying to hide from him.

He also found the missing fuck.

Dead on the warehouse floor in a pool of his own blood. The guy's face was blown off from the chin upward. He still had one eyeball left, but it was half hanging out of his face, and half resting in brain matter splattered on his cheek and the concrete.

Jesus Christ.

"S-s-s-sorry," the idiot with the gun mumbled. "I d-d-didn't mean t-t-t-o. I j-j-just—it went off! I w-w-waved it, and—"

"Figured out how to get the bullets in, did you?"

The guy swallowed his next reply instead of speaking and stuttering even more than he already was. He could probably tell just by Cross's cold, calm demeanor that he was in for a world of trouble if he didn't *shut up right now*.

Smart, really.

Cross was too exhausted for this today. He really just wanted to go home, and salvage the rest of this awful fucking day with his wife and kids.

Anything but this.

He wasn't asking for a lot.

Coming close enough that he could snatch the gun away—Cross really couldn't afford to have the idiot shooting someone else at the moment—he removed the weapon, and felt slightly safer with it being in his own grasp.

"What did you think would happen if you waved a loaded gun around?" Cross asked.

"I … don't know," the guy said lamely.

"You don't know."

It wasn't even a question.

"No—"

Before the guy could even finish his sentence, Cross lifted the rifle, and pulled the trigger. The bullet tore through the fool's face, and sent his head snapping back in the most morbid way with a sickening crack. Blood and matter spewed from the now-gaping hole in the man's face. His body quickly hit the floor with a dull thud.

Dead.

Just like that.

Easy.

Two less fucks for the world.

Cross felt no guilt. Frankly, idiots like that could not be afforded the privilege of walking and breathing the same air as other people. Or worse … spread their seed of stupid on to a new generation. Foolishness bred only more foolishness.

He considered his actions a gift to the universe, really.

Silence echoed in the warehouse after Cross shot the guy. He didn't think any of the others even took a damn breath for a whole minute or more—the first time all day that they had actually decided to close their yapping traps.

Which was smart, really.

At the moment, he was three seconds away—or less—from killing the rest of them, too. It was really only going to take one of them pushing him just the right way, and that was going to be the fucking end of it.

No excuses.

Sighing, Cross discharged the magazine from the rifle, and then removed the stock, too. Now practically useless, and not very dangerous, he set the gun on a nearby table before he faced the rest of the stunned men.

Four fucks left.

For now.

"Get out," Cross uttered.

Deathly calm.

Entirely cold.

The four didn't need to be told again. They scattered like frightened rats in a dank back alley that just had a light shined on them.

Cross didn't move until the last one was out of the front door. And only then did he pull out the phone from his slacks pocket. Dialing a familiar number, he put the phone to his ear, and listened to it ring.

Finally, the biggest Fuck of the hour picked up the phone. "Cross. How's things?"

"Andino," Cross replied dryly. "Two of your men are dead. The other four will be returned to you in small little pieces that you'll be able to put together like a puzzle for their casket viewings should you send them to me again. I hope you understand."

For a long while, Andino was silent. Then, quietly and slowly, the man started to chuckle. Cross had no fucking idea what was so funny.

"I wondered how long you would last with those idiots," Andino managed to mutter through his laughter.

"You sent them to me *knowing* what they were like?"

"I hate cleaning house," Andino admitted. "Plus, some of them might have just needed a good scare to set them straight. You're good for both things."

Rage swelled through Cross.

"Andino?"

"What?"

"If you ever waste my time again, I will cut your fucking heart out, and mail it to your wife while it's still fresh enough to bleed when she opens it up. The next men you send to me for this better be more than worth my ass getting out of bed. Under-fucking-stood?"

Andino sighed. "Well, you're no fun."

"Don't *ever* fuck with me and my guns again."

19

The Mother

Cece POV

"I miss when you were younger," Catherine said.

Cece peered up from the tablet in her hands to find her mother staring at her from across the aisle of the private jet. Other than the dark hair and brown eyes she had taken from her father, looking at her mother was like staring into an older mirror. A reflection of herself stared back—the same bow-shaped lips, delicate features, high cheekbones, and wide eyes.

"Why?" Cece asked.

Catherine smiled softly. "Things were simpler—easier, maybe. When I had to pick up and go for business, I could just take you right along with me. You were always happy to go, too. Now, you're thirteen, have school, and—"

"You could always homeschool me," Cece suggested.

Her mother lifted a single, perfectly manicured brow high. "Really?"

Cece made a face. "Well, maybe not. I guess I wouldn't get to see most of my friends nearly as much as I do now."

"If ever," Catherine added.

"Yeah."

Catherine gave a little sigh, and stared out the port window of the plane. "I know you're pretty set on … doing this with me. Being like me, I mean."

Her mother was always careful with her words. She chose each statement she made like someone might overhear it. Cece had become used to communicating this way with her ma—and even her dad—over the years.

It was just their way.

Their life.

"This is all I ever wanted, Ma," Cece said.

To be like her mom.

And her grandmother before her, too.

A Queen Pin—*the* queen.

It was in Cece's blood. It was what she was born to do. This was her birthright. She had grown up under the feet of some of the most powerful and amazing woman she had ever known. Her mother and grandmother commanded.

They ruled.

They were feared.

Respected.

"Maybe this is all you've ever wanted to do," Catherine replied, "because it's also the only thing you have ever known, Cece. Have you ever considered that side of the coin?"

Cece shrugged. "So?"

Her mother laughed lightly, and glanced upward. "So, my little smartass, I feel like you might be a bit biased."

Again … so?

Cece just stared at her mother, and said nothing. Catherine continued to stare right back entirely unfazed.

"Do you know that I am trying to let you have as normal of a life as I can possibly give you?" her mother asked. "High school, prom, friends, boys … I want you to enjoy these things, Cece. I want you to appreciate having these experiences, and this time before your focus changes to business entirely."

Because it would happen.

Eventually.

Cece heard what her mother didn't say.

"I know, Ma," Cece said.

Catherine looked back out the window. "Good."

"Isn't that strange, though?"

"Hmm?"

"That you miss when I was little, and you could take me everywhere. But now you kind of wish that I would slow down. That's what you mean, right?"

Catherine's smile was soft as she looked back at her daughter. "Yeah, that's what I mean."

"So is it—strange?"

"Normal, I think. All things considered."

Cece smiled, too. "You know, Ma, if you asked me to choose any other normal thing, or the chance to be with you ... I would pick you."

"You would, huh?"

"Always. You're my ma."

Catherine was quiet for a long time, but her gaze never drifted away from Cece for even a second. She could tell her mother was trying to find something when she looked at her—something that wasn't clearly visible, but had to be there, nonetheless.

It was not the first time her mother did something like that. Sometimes, when Cece was hiding a secret, it was like her mother just knew she was holding something back simply by looking at her.

"What?" Cece asked.

Catherine shook her hear. "I was just thinking that years ago, this could have been me and your grandmamma. Different circumstances, though. Entirely different."

Oh.

Now she was really curious.

Her mother and grandmother didn't talk a lot about how exactly Catherine had come into the business with Catrina. Cece always just assumed it was like her and her ma—she grew up in it all, saw the business happening around her, and naturally, gravitated toward the same path because this was what she was meant for.

Was it the same for her ma?

Cece leaned forward a bit in the seat, unable to hide her curiosity. "Why is it different?"

Catherine waved a hand between them. "When I was *your* age, I used to have to snoop through my mother's office and things just to find out any little detail about her life beyond the woman who ran our household. She was my mother—my father's wife. She was the woman who tucked me into bed, and read me stories."

"But?"

"But I also knew that wasn't the end of her tale. I knew she was more—something else entirely when she left our home for weeks at a time. But whenever I would ask, she shot me down. She didn't want me to know what she was doing, or who she was."

Cece frowned. "But why?"

That didn't sound like her grandmamma at all.

"I guess because my mother wanted to be one thing to me, Cece. Just my *mother*. And she thought hiding things or refusing to indulge my curiosity in this business would be enough to keep me away from it."

Cece's brow furrowed. "Clearly it didn't."

"Nope."

"So, she ... changed, I guess?"

"Nope," her mother repeated, laughed. "My cousins brought me in on their business. I was a dealer behind my parents' backs for years. A decade, probably, before they found out. I was into my twenties when my mother finally got that this was what I was good at—college wasn't for me, and I wasn't going to be anybody's dumb little house wife turning cheek to their business. No, I was meant to be ... something else. Something more like my mother."

"A queen," Cece said.

Catherine stared at her daughter, silent.

Cece stared right back.

"Like me and you," Cece added quieter.

"Is it like me and you?"

"I know what I want, Ma."

And Cece could only hope that someday, she would be just like her mother—that she would stand tall and proud like her mother.

Beautiful. Magnificent. Amazing.

Strong. Powerful. Resilient.

Smart. Refined. Elegant.

"You will be," Catherine said, as though she could read her daughter's mind.

"What, Ma?"

"Amazing—like the ones who came before you, Cece."

Cece had big shoes to fill.

It didn't scare her one bit.

20

The Crush

Cece POV

"Oh, good," Cece's mother said as the two came to the exit door of the plane. "Miguel made it in time. I hate when I have to call in a driver."

Cece followed her mother out of the plane, and found Catherine's right-hand man wasn't waiting alone. He'd brought along his oldest son—Juan.

Instantly, a hot flush climbed up thirteen-year-old Cece's cheeks, and then raced down her throat as she caught sight of Juan leaning against the black Mercedes.

It wasn't even her first time seeing Juan. She had known him for practically her entire life. He was two years older than her—fifteen—but he never made Cece feel like the annoying little girl he got stuck looking after whenever their parents had to do business.

They were friends.

Sort of.

Cece didn't know when—or how—it happened, but sometime over the last year, she stopped seeing Juan like just a friend. Maybe it happened while he was growing taller, and filling out. Or maybe it was when his dark eyes started to always follow her whenever she moved.

It could have just been the fact Cece started noticing boys in general. Juan just ended up being the only boy she really cared to notice.

He was handsome, too.

Russet skin, and amber eyes. A baseball player with the grace and agility to prove it, not to mention the body ...

Embarrassment crept up Cece's cheeks again.

Dammit.

"Cece?"

It was only her mother saying her name that brought Cece out of her head. Apparently, she had all but come to a standstill on the bottom of the jet's stairs.

Probably while staring.

At Juan.

Ugh.

"Yeah, Ma?"

Catherine glanced up the stairs to the jet, and then back to her daughter. "Did you forget something on the plane?"

"No," Cece said quickly.

"Is something wrong?"

Cece's gaze darted over her mother's shoulder to see Juan talking to his father. "No, Ma, nothing is wrong."

Just a little awkward.

The butterflies were back in her belly, too.

God.

Catherine followed her daughter's gaze and then she grinned. "Ah."

That stupid blush came back again at full force. She could actually feel the way the blood rushed to the surface of her skin to show off her shame. She might as well have just turned into a goddamn tomato for as red as she probably was.

Cece tried to play it off by coming down the last steps, and pushing past her stone-still mother. Because what else could she do?

"Leave it alone, Ma," Cece said.

Catherine laughed, and grabbed her daughter's wrist to keep Cece from going any further. She pulled hard to swing Cece around. Like this, Cece had no choice but to look her mother in the face—Catherine could see everything Cece was trying to hide, then.

"Wait a minute," her mother said. "So ... Juan, huh?"

Cece made a face. "It's just a stupid crush."

"Does he know?"

Her laughter tasted a little too bitter on her tongue.

"Ma, I don't think he notices me at all."

Catherine frowned, and took one step closer to her daughter. The way they were positioned kept Cece from view of Juan and Miguel.

Well, her face.

They could only see her back.

"Hey, now," Catherine said.

"What?"

"Look at me."

Cece did.

Catherine winked. "You are too beautiful, and far too amazing for someone to overlook you. You stand out—you fucking *shine*."

Cece grinned.

Her mom nodded. "And trust me, Juan notices you, too, Cece."

"You think?"

"I *know* he does, but I also know he's a decent young man with his head on straight, and his heart in the right place."

"What does that even mean?"

Catherine bent down to stare Cece head-on at eye-level. "It means ... you won't be thirteen forever, but right now you are—he knows it."

Oh.

"Now," her mom said, "smile."

Cece did.

"And go say hello," Catherine added. "He's just a boy at the end of the day. And you? You are the most amazing girl. Got it?"

She nodded. "Got it, Ma."

A little pep talk from her mom went a long way when it came to Cece. Catherine seemed to know just what to say, or just what Cece needed to hear to make everything better somehow no matter what.

She loved her ma.

Always.

The two crossed the tarmac to where Miguel and Juan broke out of their conversation to greet them. Juan turned a blinding smile on Cece the moment her eyes met his.

Jesus.

Were crushes supposed to make you feel lightheaded?

She didn't get the chance to think on it for long. Once she was close enough, Juan took the chance to wrap an arm around her neck, and then he pulled her in for a tight hug that all but took her breath away for a quick second.

Strong arms.

Woodsy scent.

Cece's heart skipped beats.

"Hey, Cece," Juan murmured into her hair. "I missed you, my girl."

Maybe it was the whole *my girl* thing that caused this mess that was Cece's heart, too.

Yep.

Much more than a little crush.

Cece's face was going to permanently settle into a scowl if she couldn't get her raging jealousy under control. It didn't help that Juan seemed entirely oblivious to Cece's growing frustrations ten feet away.

Light, girlish giggles brought Cece out of her thoughts. Sure enough, she found the girl, who had approached Juan from the moment he and Cece came down to the hotel's pool, was the owner of the stupid laughter.

Why did girls think giggling was cute?

Child-like giggles.

It wasn't cute.

The girl was pretty, though.

Blue-eyed.

Peach and cream skin.

Blonde hair.

Total Cali girl.

Everything opposite to Cece.

Older, too.

Fifteen, or sixteen.

"You should come," the girl said. "Oh, my God. I bet you would have so much fun with us, Juan."

Juan shot a glance over his shoulder at Cece. She quickly turned her head to pretend she wasn't listening to their conversation. He probably still saw her doing it.

"Uh," Juan started to say.

Cece looked back just in time to see the girl reach out and place her palm against Juan's pec. The girl's white bikini was so small, it might as well not even be there at all.

Jealousy burned through Cece even hotter.

"I would really like it if you would come," the girl said.

Cece wouldn't blame Juan at all if he went with the pretty girl and her giggling friends waiting at the other side of the pool. He was closer to them in age, and they probably had better plans other than sitting poolside all day.

Screw it.

Cece grabbed her earbuds for her tablet, and shoved them in. If she couldn't force herself to ignore them, then she would just drown their conversation out with loud music. She refused to even look in their direction after that.

Childish?

Maybe a bit.

It was better than her going over there to try and rip the girl's blonde hair out of her head. Besides, she didn't think Juan would like that very much.

Especially if he liked the girl.

Crap.

What if he did actually like her?

That kind of made Cece's heart hurt.

This crush thing sucked.

All of the sudden, the sounds of the pool filled Cece's ears as her earbuds were tugged away. A shadow darkened over her form as Juan came to stand next to her reclining lounger.

"Hey," he said.

Cece tried not to frown. "Hey. I guess you're going to hang out with your new friend, huh?"

Juan's brow dipped. "No way, Cece."

Her heart perked.

Stupid, traitorous heart.

"No?" she dared to ask.

He grinned. "Nope—today's all for you. I promised."

"Yeah, you did."

"You okay?"

Cece glanced over at where the girl had rejoined her friends. "I am now."

Juan nodded. "Huh."

"What?"

"You look like you smelled something bad."

Cece shrugged. "No, I just—"

"I didn't mean to make you jealous."

Her first instinct was to deny his words—she didn't want him to know she liked him that way, partly. Another part of her *did* want him to know exactly that.

This teenaged girl thing was *hard*.

The way Juan looked at her made Cece stop and think before she said anything at all. She thought about her mom, too, and what Catherine always told her.

Petty girls made scenes.

Petty girls lie.

Petty girls play games.

Queens didn't need or do those things.

"I don't like seeing you with other girls," Cece settled on saying.

Juan dropped into the lounger beside hers. "All right."

"All right," she echoed.

He looked over at her, saying, "It's always just me and you when it's us, Cece. I promise."

Her daddy once told her to find a boy who kept his promises because those were the kinds of boys who grew up to be good men.

She knew that she had found that boy.

Juan.

They still had years to go yet, though.

21

The Guns

Cross POV

Cross wasn't the type to have spells of bad days. A day here or there, maybe. Something that put him on edge, and made getting through the day a taxing event. Everybody occasionally dealt with something like that.

But several?

In a row?

That just wasn't Cross's style. And yet, that was exactly how he had been feeling for almost two weeks now. Like there was some kind of shitty mood he just couldn't seem to shake. A stink to his mind that was clouding up everything else around him.

The proverbial rain cloud was following him around day in and day out.

How fucking cliché.

Cross drove into his Newport garage, and was surprised to see his ten-year-old son's head pop up from under the hood of Catherine's car. He gave his son a look when their gazes locked through the windshield.

Naz should have been in school.

Although, Cross supposed he really wasn't all that surprised to see Naz under the hood of a car tinkering. The kid was good with his hands. He had been taking shit apart since he learned how to walk. It took a few years for Naz to learn how to put things back together, though.

Naturally, Naz's interests moved to focus on certain things. At only ten, he could rebuild a carburetor, or an engine. He had mastered the art of rebuilds on old, vintage cars—something Cross thanked Zeke for.

His boy could fix just about any electronic that was put into his hands, and he was already beginning to code. He liked to spend time with one of Cross's guys who had a knack for hacking. Something Naz found challenging enough to keep his attention for longer than five seconds.

And all of this?

It was before Cross even got into Naz's taste for guns, sports, and more.

Yeah, there was more.

Cross had to keep Naz busy—constantly. Otherwise, trouble found Nazio quickly when he was bored, or worse, his hands were left idle for too long.

It also probably explained why his son wasn't at school at the moment. Likely. He got bored. They sent him home.

Naz was smart—too damn smart. *Gifted* kind of smart.

Every parent thought their kid was a special little star. No other kid could compare to their child. Sure, Cross thought the same thing about his kids, too.

The difference?

Naz *was* an intellectual fucking star.

His IQ tested on part with Albert Einstein.

Add in a heavy dose of arrogance, a touch of swag, and those goddamn Donati genes to give him good looks, and Naz was trouble walking. Thank fuck, puberty was still a couple of years away yet.

It was the only thing saving them.

Karma had come hard for Cross.

Damn, he loved his kids, though.

Cross stepped out of the Rolls-Royce, and rested his arms along the roof as Naz approached. His son was still all tall legs, and long arms, but he would fill out soon enough.

"What did they do—send you home again?" Cross asked.

Naz wiped his hands down on a rag. "With another stupid pamphlet for that school."

Cross frowned at the way Naz twisted his words when he spoke about the school for gifted children. The district, his teachers, principal, and more had been pushing this goddamn institution on Naz and his parents since shortly after he entered Pre-K, and they realized he was not like the other kids as far as intelligence went.

Maturity-wise, though?

Naz was just like every other kid his age. He was not suddenly ahead of every other ten year old in most other aspects—except for intelligence—simply because he was brilliant. Sure, he could memorize everything he ever looked at and read, but he was still just ten years old.

Still a boy.

Naz didn't want the special school. He wanted to remain with his friends—with kids his own age that he had known since being a toddler. Being around other kids who were brilliant like him didn't really appeal to Naz, either, when the adults around him tried using that like dangling bait as a reason to get him to enroll in the school for the gifted.

Just because Naz was a fucking genius—by all measurable standards—didn't mean he was also socially awkward, and needed to be put away with other people *like him*.

Quite the opposite.

People *flocked* to his boy. Naz also wasn't so arrogant about his intelligence that he shoved it in other people's faces like some might.

In fact, he never did that at all.

To those who didn't know Naz, he seemed like a regular kid doing his own thing. It was only once someone spent a little bit of time with him, and saw him at work did they realize, *holy shit, this kid is something else.*

"To be fair," Naz said as he tossed the rag away to a nearby metal table, "I did hand in every assignment the math teacher had planned for the rest of the year."

Cross's brow shot up high. "School just started three weeks ago, Naz."

When did his kid even find time to do that?

Oh, yeah.

His boy slept four hours, and acted like it was a ten-hour sleep.

Naz shrugged. "Yeah, well …"

"How did you even get the list of assignments the teacher had planned? And for the whole year? *Really*?"

His son looked away at that question. "Plausible deniability."

"Naz," Cross warned.

"The assignments were on a district sheet of what they *must* teach—what the students must learn from semester to semester. The shit they test us on, you know. They even have assignments they must give out to us—they have to follow it, Dad. Maybe I hacked into the teacher's—"

"*Naz!*"

"In hindsight," Naz said, holding up a hand, "that was a bad idea."

"You think?"

"I can tell Jaz that I got hacking down, though," Naz said, grinning.

Cross sighed. "So did you get sent home, or did you get expelled?"

"Two-week suspension."

"Oh, Naz, that's going to go on your record."

He didn't really give a shit that Naz got suspended. He cared that hacking into the computer system would be listed as a reason why.

"Actually, I think they might let me work on coding their security, and conveniently drop that little part on my suspension form," Naz said.

Huh.

"Well, all right."

Naz smiled, and tugged his ever-present beanie from his head. "The gun run was today, right?"

Instantly, Cross's bad mood was back. "Yeah."

He ran the gunrunning operation for the Marcello family. He simply didn't run the guns anymore.

"How did it go?" his son asked.

Naz's excitement and interest was so bright and clear, that it made Cross smile. Just because he was in a pissy mood about once again sending the guys off on a run that he couldn't join didn't mean he had to pass that over onto his son, too.

"So far, so good. I don't expect to hear anything more from them until the guns land in port, and they're onto the next phase."

As usual.

They would be successful.

He trained them, after all.

His team was Ace.

And all too often—like today—Cross wished he was out there with them on the run, too. He missed the rush he used to get from it. The thrill it provided like none other. Being the man behind the scenes, was not quite the same thing as being the man behind the wheel, so to speak.

He didn't regret his choice to stop running guns for even a second, of course. His reason for quitting back then had been more than valid, and appropriate. He had been too hot of a figure in the North American gunrunning scene to continue. He was—essentially—a loaded gun ready to blow. Every run he took after that last one was playing with fire. It would only be a matter of time until he had gotten caught.

Cross was not willing to take that risk when it meant he might end up leaving his wife and children without him while he spent twenty to life behind bars for some fucking guns. His family, and *their* life, would always be worth far more than gun metal, and a goddamn thrill.

But ... nostalgia could be a mean bitch.

Hence, his bad mood.

Cross opted to change the subject back to the school thing with his son as to get his mind and mood away from gunrunning. "How mad is your mother about this suspension?"

"She gave me that look."

Cross laughed.

Yeah, every mother had that look.

"All right. Thanks, son."

He patted his son on the head as he passed him.

"Hey, Dad?"

"Yeah, Naz?"

"When can I go on a run, too?"

Cross turned on his heel to eye Naz. "Not at ten."

"Eleven?"

Jesus.

"Give me a line here, kiddo."

Naz rolled his eyes. "Thirteen, then."

"Eighteen," Cross countered, "and I want to see some direction in school other than you getting suspended every couple of months."

"Sixteen."

Man, this kid …

"Fuck no, Naz."

"*Sixteen*," Naz repeated, "and I will *try* that school. Try, Dad."

Cross's brow flew up. "You know that your mother and I—"

"I know I don't have to go to it."

"Good … okay, as long as you know that." Cross scrubbed a hand down his jaw, and decided on another offer for his son. "Seventeen—sixteen *only* if you graduate early."

"You know I could graduate by thirteen."

"Cece will be in her final year, though."

Naz scowled. "Fine—seventeen, but sixteen if I graduate early."

Cross knew throwing Cece in there would keep Naz in line. He was way too protective of his older sister. The idea of her still being in school while Naz was not would drive him practically insane.

"You can quit that school whenever you want, and return to a normal district," Cross said.

Naz nodded. "Good because I probably will."

Cross chuckled. "Just … finish school, son. Get some years under you yet. You have got lots of time to figure out the rest. What if you end up wanting to be a scientist—or even a surgeon?"

Naz made a face. "I don't think those things are in my blood."

"You can do *anything*—blood or not."

"Can I?"

Why did this conversation feel so familiar to Cross?

Ah, yes.

Because this had once been him with his father. And the words Calisto had told Cross all those years ago were still very present in his mind. He never forgot them because they validated everything he knew about his father, and the love the man had for him.

And that was all *before* he even knew the truth about his paternity.

"Naz, you can *be* anything. You are that amazing. And I am going to be proud regardless of what you do because you are mine, and that's never going to change. You don't have to be like me, son."

Naz smirked a bit. "I'm too unique to be *you*."

Yeah.

A fucking star.

"So, deal?" Naz asked.

Cross nodded. "Deal."

Cross found his wife sitting in her library. She didn't look up from her laptop as he took a seat beside her on the couch.

"Did you talk to Naz?"

"He told me what happened," Cross replied, leaning back into the cushions and staring at the ceiling. "Amongst other things."

"What other things?"

"He's going to run guns."

Catherine passed him a look. "He's *ten*."

Cross shrugged. "I can see it."

"How was work?"

"Terrible. The run is going wonderfully. The guys are great. Money is coming in."

"And that's terrible, huh?"

"I hate being the man behind the scenes, Catty," Cross murmured. "I want to be the one running the guns. Nothing new, babe."

Catherine frowned. "The king in the shadows."

"Something like that."

"It won't be that way forever, Cross."

"What?"

Catherine shook her head, and smiled in that knowing way of hers.

"What?" he asked again.

"Someone is going to have to teach Naz. *You*. I know you, Cross—you're never going to sit on the sidelines when it comes to Naz. You never have. You *can't*."

Cross grinned. "Probably not, no."

"See."

"You're not mad at the idea I might start up again? It was you who wanted me to stop, after all."

"Ten years ago," Catherine said. "Enough time has passed."

"Have I told you how much I love you lately?"

Catherine rolled her pretty eyes. "Yes, but tell me again."

Cross leaned over on the couch, caught his wife's chin in his hand, and pulled her in for a searing kiss. "I found the most perfect woman for me—you. My wife who always knows what's in my head, and where I need to go.

Usually before I even know it."

"You do that for me, too," Catherine pointed out.

"Maybe, but ... I don't know, I needed this."

"What, this chat?"

"With you, yeah. About everything."

Catherine laughed. "We certainly don't need you finding trouble because you're *bored*. Sound familiar?"

So, yeah.

That was true, too.

Naz got it honestly.

All that crazy intelligence shit came from God, though.

22

The Brother

Cece/Naz POV

Cece hid in the treehouse she hadn't actually played in since she was a girl. Once, she had gone to a friend's house as a child, and saw that they had a beautiful doll-like designed treehouse just for them.

Despite the fact that Cece hadn't been very interested in playing as a child, like most other children her age, she had wanted a treehouse for herself something awful. She went home that day after visiting her friend, and told her father what she wanted.

Her father had one built before the week was out.

That was years ago, now.

She wasn't so little anymore being fourteen. She had definitely outgrown the age where she should be playing in something like a treehouse.

And yet, she still used it.

It was still her safe place.

Sometimes, like today, it was just the kind of place she needed. It gave her somewhere to disappear to—so she could be totally alone.

Here, she wouldn't have to explain to her mom or dad why she was crying.

It was stupid, anyway.

A stupid thing to cry over.

That was one of the many things that sucked about being fourteen. Or rather, being a fourteen-year-old girl.

Sometimes, stupid things made her cry.

"Cece?" she heard her father call out. "Supper is ready!"

Cece quickly wiped the tears from her face. "Okay, Daddy."

"You okay?"

God.

Did he hear the tears in her voice, or something?

He always knew when something was wrong.

"I'm fine, Daddy," she called back.

"If you're sure …"

"I'm sure."

Her father must have believed her because she heard the back door to their house close a few seconds later. She chose to stay where she was for a couple of more minutes in the treehouse. Long enough to dry her face, and make sure her eyes wouldn't be red.

Cece was just getting ready to stand up when Naz popped his head up over the bottom of the doorway. Apparently, he climbed up the ladder without Cece hearing a damn thing. Like a little mouse or something.

Not surprising.

Naz was sneaky like that.

"What are you doing?" Naz asked.

"Nothing."

Her ten-year-old brother's gaze narrowed. "You sure?"

"Yeah, I guess."

Naz climbed up the last couple of steps, and pushed his body into the treehouse. He sat down right in front of the door so that Cece couldn't get past him at all.

"Supper is ready," he said.

"So move, and we can go eat," Cece replied.

Naz cocked a brow, and then shook his head. "Nah, I don't think so."

"You're super annoying, Naz."

He only shrugged.

Cece sat back down. "How was school?"

"Boring," her brother muttered, "like always."

Naz was crazy smart. People liked to toss around the word genius, but he didn't really like being called that. At least, not to his face. He was so smart, though, that he could do Cece's math and science homework—with a guaranteed A.

"So, what's wrong?" Naz asked.

Cece shook her head. "Nothing, Naz."

"Yeah, except you only come up to the treehouse when something is wrong. Like the last time—it was because Ma had to go to Cali last minute, and wouldn't take you with her. So you sulked up here for half the damn day."

"I do not sulk!"

"Okay," Naz drawled.

"I don't, Naz."

"Point is, this is where you go when you're upset. So—"

"It's just something little and stupid," she said, wishing he would drop it.

Naz frowned. "Is it stupid if it made you cry?"

"I'm not—"

"I know what you look like after you cry, Cece."

Of course, he did.

Cece's very first best friend had been her little brother. He looked out for her even though he was four years younger than her. Sometimes, he could be the typical, annoying little brother that never left her alone. Other times, he was the only person Cece cared to share her secrets with at all.

"It's really nothing, Naz," she told him.

Mostly, she just didn't want her brother worrying, or getting pissed off.

"Want me to tell Dad that I found you upset?"

Cece scowled. "Blackmail, really?"

Naz smiled, and tipped his head down so that the top of his beanie was all she could see instead of his face. "It's what I do."

Well … crap.

"A guy I don't even like called me ugly," Cece muttered.

She kept her gaze on her hands instead of her brother.

"He wanted me to send him a picture, and I wouldn't, so he called me ugly."

"A picture?" Naz made a noise in the back of his throat. "What's he need a picture of?"

Cece glanced up, and gave her brother a look. "You're really smart, but sometimes, Naz, you're also kind of clueless."

"Hey!"

"What kind of picture, Naz, *really*?"

Naz looked upwards, and made a face. "Oh, like a bad one? Like … a naked one?"

"Basically, yeah."

She knew better than to be sending pictures of herself like that to *anybody*. For one, because it was wrong. And for two, her father and mother would kill her if they ever found out.

"And he called you ugly?" Naz asked. "Just because of that?"

"It's not that he called me ugly—that's not why I am upset."

And she knew she wasn't ugly, either. She took after her mother, and Ma was the most beautiful woman Cece knew.

"It just ... sucked," Cece said lamely. "He had to seem cool, or whatever, when I told him, so he tried to hurt me, I guess. Like I said, that just sucks, and it's stu—"

"Not stupid," Naz interjected. "I'm sorry the guy's a jerk."

Cece smiled. "Make sure you never make girls cry, Naz."

Naz nodded. "Promise. By the way ..."

"Yeah?"

"Who was the guy?"

Naz POV

"Hey, Zeke?"

"Yeah, *principe*?"

His father's best friend and right-hand man was the one tasked with driving Naz to school today. Sometimes it was an enforcer if everybody else was busy for whatever reason. More often than not, it was his mother or father.

But his dad had business in Hell's Kitchen, and his mom had to fly out to California over the weekend.

So that left Zeke.

Naz liked Zeke.

"Do you gotta knife, or something?" Naz asked.

Zeke side-eyed him from the driver's seat. "What in the fuck do you need a knife for?"

"Just because."

"Naz."

"Plausible deniability," Naz added.

"Jesus, kid."

"Well?"

Zeke scowled. "Are you going to kill someone?"

"No."

"Cause property damage?"

"Try real hard not to," Naz returned, though that was probably a lie.

Zeke grunted under his breath. "You get caught, then you didn't get it from me, understand?"

"Swear on my life," Naz promised.

"In the dash, *principe*."

Sure enough, Naz found a switch blade in the dash. He flicked the blade out, and tested the sharpness of the edge with the pad of his thumb. Satisfied it would handle the business he needed it for, Naz slipped the blade into his pocket.

"Remember our deal," Zeke said.

Naz nodded. "You got it, *zio*."

Zeke wasn't his real uncle, but he still loved him like he was.

Soon, Zeke was pulling up to the drop-off line for the lower and upper Academy. Naz said goodbye to Zeke, and stepped out of the car with his backpack tossed over his shoulder. He could see Cece on the steps of the upper Academy talking to one of her friends. She almost always traveled to school with one of her older friends.

Naz waited for Zeke to pull out of the line, and then drive out of the parking lot before he headed for the upper Academy. Or rather, the parking lot the upper Academy students used.

Cece had given Naz the name of the guy.

Teller Masterson.

Stupid fucking name.

Naz asked some friends—Teller was a senior in the upper Academy. What he was doing asking a fourteen year old to send him pictures was anybody's guess.

He sounded like a creep.

Soon, Naz found the car he was looking for, and the dick it belonged to.

Teller.

The guy leaned against the side of the car, and smoked a cigarette. He gave Naz a passing look, likely not recognizing him.

That was okay.

He would know him after this.

"Aren't you on the wrong side of the Academy, kid?" Teller asked.

Naz smirked. "It's Naz."

He didn't give the guy a chance to respond—instead pulling out that switchblade from his pocket, flicking out the blade, and ramming it hard into the guy's back tire. All the way to the fucking hilt so the tire was ruined.

"Hey, what the fuck?"

Teller came closer.

Naz yanked the blade out, and pointed it at Teller. "Next time, it'll be your fucking throat."

"Wh-what?"

Yeah.

Naz bet it was some kind of messed up shit to be threatened by a ten year old. But ... Naz was Naz. He had a mind like lightning—electric, fast, and growing more dangerous by the day. He was a Donati, and his life was not anything like this rich, spoiled brat's life. The first time he saw a man die—he was *seven*. The guy shouldn't have pulled a gun on his dad.

That's just how it went.

"My name is Nazio Donati," Naz said quietly, "and make sure you get it right when you spread it around. You ever fuck with my sister—Cece—again, and they won't be able to put all the pieces of you back together once I am done with you. Just so we're clear, asshole."

With that, Naz walked away.

Teller didn't follow.

23

The Boy

Catherine POV

Catherine stayed to the edges of the room and kept a close watch on the most interesting part of her fifteen-year-old daughter's birthday celebration. Cece didn't want to call it a birthday party because apparently, that just sounded too juvenile for her.
Whatever.
A *celebration* it was.
The house was decorated. The family had come. Cece's friends had poured into the house to fill it full. Presents were waiting on a table—piled nearly to the ceiling in beautiful wrapping paper with sparkling bows.
A cake needed to be cut.
And yet, Catherine had other things to do at the moment. Better things, even.
Well, depending on who you asked ...
"What are you doing over here in the corner by yourself?"
Catherine gave her mother a look, and put a finger to her lips. "Shhh, look."
Catrina did, and found the same scene that Catherine had been keeping an eye on all night. Actually, if she were being honest, this whole

thing was years in the making for Cece. It was only now that the distance was starting to close between youthful, innocent crushes to something entirely different.

"Oh," Catrina said.

Catherine nodded. "Yeah."

Across the room, Cece stood chatting with a group of her friends. Standing close behind her was Juan—Miguel's oldest son. He had a plate of food in his hands, and every so often, offered Cece a bite to take from his fingertips.

It was sweet.

It seemed innocent.

Except her daughter smiled in *that way* every single time she took a bite. Cece was constantly checking over her shoulder to make sure Juan had not gone too far from her side. And if another girl tried stepping in Juan's path during the evening?

Nope.

Cece stopped that *fast*.

"How long has this been going on?" Catrina asked. "You didn't tell me anything about *this*, Catherine."

"Because you're a gossip, Ma."

Catrina poked Catherine hard in the back. "Lies."

"Ouch."

"Well!"

Gazes moved in their direction, and Catherine turned fast to make sure her daughter didn't see her spying. She didn't want Cece to know that she was keeping an eye on these new developments between her and Juan.

"Stop looking," Catherine hissed at her mother.

Catrina rolled her eyes. "She's not even looking this way. She's too busy glaring at some girl who keeps looking at Juan."

"Really?"

Catherine turned around to look again.

Her mother had been lying.

Sort of.

Cece wasn't looking at them, but she wasn't glaring at anybody, either. No, currently, she was holding onto Juan's wrists as the two of them talked. The seventeen-year-old boy barely gave anyone else around them any of his attention while he and Cece conversed together.

She was all he cared to see.

Only she mattered.

Catherine's smile grew.

"You're very invested in this ... thing," Catrina said.

Catherine shot her mother a look. "What, like you weren't invested in my relationships as a teenager?"

"Supportive. Encouraging. I wouldn't say *invested* is the right word."

"I am those things, too, Ma."

"Uh-huh."

"Thirteen," Catherine said.

Catrina raised a brow. "I beg your pardon?"

"She has had a crush on him since she was thirteen, Ma. And Juan was always ... really sweet, and good to her. I overheard Miguel telling him once that Juan had to be respectful and not overstep his boundaries with Cece because she was two years younger than him, and it wouldn't look right for a boy his age to be chasing after a girl her age."

"I suppose that makes sense."

"He listened, too," Catherine added. "But she's not thirteen anymore, Ma."

Catrina laughed in that way of hers. "You *are* way too invested in this."

Catherine shrugged.

Oh, well.

She made no apologies.

"Someone has to be."

"Couldn't you share this investment of yours with your husband?" Catrina asked.

Catherine fake pouted. "God, Ma, why do you have to ruin everything?"

"How did I ruin it?"

"Just ..." Catherine turned to look for Cece and Juan again, but it seemed the two had disappeared. Not the other friends, though. Cece's little group of girls were still in full teenage girl mode in their semi-circle. Cece and Juan, though? Gone. "Where did they go?"

"Catherine, let them have time alone. You know, like I used to do for *you*."

She gave her mother a look. "I'm not ... getting in their business, Ma."

"Spying is the same—"

"Did you see where they went, or not?"

Catrina sighed, and rolled her eyes. "They went into the back hallway. I am going to go find your father. *He* knows how to mind his business."

"Whatever, Ma."

Catherine was already leaving her mother behind. She moved through the chatting people, and slipped into the back hallway at the same time she heard the backdoor close. A backdoor that led out to their porch.

Soon, Catherine had slipped into Cross's music room, and was peering out the window to check on her daughter there. Cece and Juan were sitting on the porch swing—fingers woven tightly together, and swinging back and forth.

Still quite innocent.

Still closing distance.

That was enough for her, really.

Catherine stepped back away from the window, done with her spying. She really didn't mean to intrude on her daughter, or anything like that. She was simply excited for Cece because she knew how long her daughter had been waiting for something like this to happen.

"Catty?"

Catherine nearly fell over her own two feet as she spun around. Cross stood in the music room's doorway with a cocked brow. "Hi. Hey. Wh—"

"What are you doing?"

"Nothing."

Cross gave her a look. "Right, okay."

"Come on, let's—"

Cross rocked back on his heels a bit, and peered out the back door. He probably had the perfect view of his daughter and Juan sitting together. Holding hands.

Catherine looked out her window.

Oh, wonderful.

They were *kissing* now.

A quick kiss.

Nothing more.

Cece initiated it, by the looks of things. And she quickly pulled away too with a sly little grin, and a laugh Catherine could only see, but not quite hear.

Oh.

"Spying, I think," Cross murmured.

Catherine looked back to her husband. "Sorry."

"You didn't think to tell me?"

"*I'm* not even supposed to know, really."

"Ah."

Catherine moved away from the window lest the two outside notice her, and came closer to her husband. Cross, despite being very protective of Cece when it came to boys and dating, seemed to be doing okay at the moment.

Maybe that was the most surprising thing of all.

"How bad do you want to go out there?" she asked him.

Cross grinned. "I'm okay, actually."

"You sure?"

"Well ... you remember the last time Miguel came to visit?"

"Last month," Catherine said. "Yeah, why?"

"Juan asked me then about taking Cece out."

Catherine's brow raised high. "And you didn't think to tell *me*?"

Cross shrugged. "I told him no."

She stiffened. "What—why?"

"Not *no* that they couldn't ... continue to be whatever the fuck they are. What are they, anyway?"

Catherine pursed her lips. "I don't know. When it's them, it's them. That's what I see, Cross. I don't worry about the rest. That's for them to figure out."

"Like us, then."

"What?"

"Us, Catty. You know, back when we were confused and together and not together ... and everything else. When it was us, we were—"

"Us," she whispered.

Cross nodded. "Yeah, babe."

"But you told him no?"

"I said no to something like them going *out* of the house alone, or that kind of thing. Besides, it's not that I don't trust Juan, Catherine. I know he would be responsible, and good to Cece."

"Then what it is?"

"Her," Cross said simply.

"Her."

"Mmhmm. She's still unsure. She still doesn't know. Last month, she was texting a boy at school, and at the last formal, she was excited about having two different boys to go with. She's still trying to figure out this dating thing—this *boys* thing. Do you want her to figure that out with him? Figure that out *on* him? A boy who cares for her—loves her?"

"You think he—"

"I know he loves her," Cross said, nodding. "And I think she loves him, too, but she's still trying to figure this out. I want her to have the time to do that, Catherine. So yeah, when it's them, it's *them*. And when it's not them, they don't have to worry about it right now."

"Huh."

"You look confused," her husband murmured, coming close enough to wrap her in his arms.

"No, not confused."

"What, then?"

"I just remembered something, that's all."

Cross tipped Catherine's head back, and dropped a kiss to her lips. "And what is that, my girl?"

"How amazing you are."

Because he was. More than anyone knew.

Except Catherine.

Catherine always knew.

24

The Date

Cross POV

"Uh … Cross?"

Cross glanced up from the work he had spread out on his desk. Plans for an outgoing shipment of illegal cigarettes and liquor to Canada. It was a damn good money maker, as far as that went.

He hated being taken away from his work, but someone was always doing that to him, anyway.

Cross found Juan standing in the doorway of his office—an eighteen year old with eyes for Cross's sixteen-year-old daughter. Although to be fair, Juan had never really stepped out of line with Cece, so to speak.

The two's interest in each other was quite clear. It had been that way since Cece was about thirteen, or so.

Juan had been raised by a decent man, though. Being that he was two years older than Cece, he didn't put holds or anything on her. He didn't pressure her, either.

Still, it was clear …
The signs were there …
It was all leading to this.
Cross knew it.

He'd been waiting for it.

"Come in, Juan," Cross said. "I didn't know you were in town."

Juan shrugged his broad shoulders—in his relaxed features, the biracial Latino-American man looked a look like his father, with just a touch of his mother, too. Handsome, definitely. He was a confident young man, and driven in his business.

He took that from his father, too.

Catherine's right-hand man, Miguel.

"Came down from California when I had a weekend off," Juan said as he took a seat across from Cross's desk. "Dad never gives me time off, so I figured I might as well take it while I could."

"Mmm, I know," Cross replied. "Cece knows it, too."

Juan's gaze drifted to the window, and then back to Cross. "Yeah, I guess."

"She misses you quite a bit when you stay gone for long periods of time."

"Don't really have a choice."

"You could try to make it a choice."

Juan glanced at Cross who only cocked a single eyebrow, and then nodded. "I will definitely do that, then."

"Good. Now, what can I do for you?"

"Do you remember when I came to speak to you last year?" Juan asked.

"I have practically watched you grow up, Juan, so yes."

"Specifically, when I asked about taking Cece out."

Cross cleared his throat. "I remember that, too, yeah."

He was not going to make this easy on the kid—well, kid was kind of insulting, considering Juan's age. But what Cross said still stood, too. He watched Juan grow up. He was always going to be somewhat of a kid to him, regardless.

That was life.

And it was really only because Cross knew Juan—and his family—so well that this entire thing was not as hard for Cross as it might have been had it been another young man sitting across from him. Someone else, and Cross would not even be willing to entertain the idea of their affections for his daughter.

Cece was ... special.

Beautiful.

Smart.

Kickass.

Badass.

Too much like her mother.

A good dose of him.

She was *theirs*.

And someone else wanted to make her theirs, too.

Juan.

"I told you to wait until she was sixteen," Cross murmured.

Juan smiled. "Her birthday is Wednesday."

"It is."

"I would like to take her out on Saturday, *if* you didn't mind, I mean."

Cross chuckled dryly. "Minding is a matter of semantics. I will always mind the thought of someone dating my daughter, but ... I also don't get a choice about the fact that she's going to grow up, and do her own thing."

"You *did* let her date other people these last couple of years."

He couldn't have missed the heat in Juan's words if he tried. Jealous, if Cross ever heard it. The thickness of Juan's jealousy colored his words heavily.

The young man didn't realize that he really had no reason to be jealous. Yes, Cece had been allowed to have boyfriends ... but better she learned to cut her teeth on a boy she would dispose of than a man who had loved her since she was just a girl.

Because Cross was not stupid.

He *knew*.

Juan loved his girl.

He had loved her for a long time.

"Not like this," Cross returned. "Boys her own age—supervised by my men, when needed. Never in a setting where a boy could drive her anywhere. They were never old enough to have a license, after all. Do you think that wasn't intentional on my part? I am not a stupid man, Juan. I have lived far more years on this earth than you have. I called those boys toys for her because that's how she treated them, and that's fine. Is that what you want to be, too—her *toy*?"

Juan's gaze flashed with something dark.

Cross smirked.

"No, I don't want to be her toy," Juan replied quietly.

"I didn't think so."

"So ..."

"So?" Cross asked.

Juan laughed. "You're not going to make this easy on me, huh?"

"Not in the least. Ask properly."

"Could I take Cece out this coming weekend, Cross? I would appreciate your blessing, and permission."

"A date, you mean."

Juan shook his head, grinning. "Yeah, a date."

"To where?"

"I was thinking Niagara Falls, actually."

Cross nodded. "Nice."

"Is that a yes, then?"

"One moment."

Cross pulled out the drawer in his desk that kept his weapons safely hidden away. He pulled out each one that was inside—a glock, an eagle, and another small handgun that was practically useless unless it was shot at close range.

He set each of the weapons on the other side of the desk one by one. It forced Juan to take a good look at each thing as Cross took his sweet ass time putting them out.

"Pick one," Cross said, leaning forward on the desk.

"Pardon?"

"Pick a gun. Whichever one you like the most, I guess."

Juan cocked a brow, but gestured at the eagle. "That one."

"Good choice."

"It's a dangerous gun."

"It is," Cross agreed. "And if you hurt my child, or if you return her to me—at any point in her life—in less than perfect condition, this is the gun I will ram down your throat before I pull the trigger."

Juan straightened in the chair.

Cross smiled. "Do you understand me?"

"Yeah, I got it."

"You sure?"

Dark brown eyes lifted to meet Cross's.

"I'd probably do it for you," Juan murmured.

Yeah, Cross knew that, too.

"Good talk, Juan," he said. "Good talk."

"Cross?"

Cross looked away from the card game he was currently having with his father, and father-in-law to find his wife standing in the kitchen entryway of their home. Catherine leaned in further with a smile, and a little nod.

"Juan is outside," Catherine said. "Are you going out to talk to him again, or are you good with letting Cece—"

"She's good to go," Cross said with a little wave. "Juan and I have talked."

Smirks passed between the men at the table. All except for one, but he wasn't quite a man yet.

Nazio, that was.

Their resident twelve-year-old genius just scowled.

Cross ignored his son, and went back to his wife. "Tell Cece to stop by and say goodbye to me before she goes, babe."

"All right."

Really, Cross just wanted to see his daughter before she went off on her first date with Juan. Give her a kiss. Reassure himself that she would be fine.

Of course, Cece would be fine. She was far too much like her mother and grandmother—with a good dose of her father, too—to be anything *but* fine. Cece could more than handle herself in a bad situation.

And ... well, she was sixteen.

Cross's daughter had started having boyfriends around fourteen, or so, but nothing that had ever been serious, and she never really seemed very interested. It seemed like his only daughter was waiting on something.

Or rather, someone.

Juan Lopez.

Cross wasn't too concerned about Juan and Cece finally beginning their ... thing. The two had certainly waited long enough, and Cross was more than aware that Juan had been very careful to respect Cross's choices and requests about his daughter. Hell, the two worked together at times—like Miguel and Catherine did—but Juan's interest in Catherine's business only went as far as Cece's involvement a lot of the time.

Funny how that worked.

With Catherine gone from the kitchen, the card game continued.

"Talked to the boy, did you?" Dante asked, smirking.

"Kind of like the way you talked to me," Cross replied.

Kind of.

Calisto passed a look between the two men. "I'm sorry—at some point you had a chat with my son when he was a teenager?"

Dante's gaze never left the cards in his hands. "Yes, he was pursuing my daughter, and had the arrogance of a ... well, you know how he was, Cal."

"And how did this *talk* go down, exactly?"

"He took me into a soundproofed room in the basement," Cross said, "and threatened me."

Dante grinned. "Fun times."

That was one way to put it. Now that Cross was the man on the other side of that equation—the father of a daughter being pursued—he understood exactly why Dante had done that to a younger him.

And he didn't blame the man.

"Anyway," Cross said, throwing his hand of cards down to fold them, "if anything, that memory of Dante and I gave me an idea for Juan when he requested to take Cece out."

Chuckles passed around the table.

All except for a still-scowling Nazio.

"I still don't like this," Naz grumbled.

Cross rolled his eyes upward. "You don't have to like it, Naz."

"She's not even going to have a chaperone!"

"She doesn't need one."

"And what if they—"

"Shut up, Naz," Cross interjected with a smile. "You do not get to decide when your sister can date, or whom she can date, for that matter. We have talked about this again and *again*. What I told you has not changed."

"Yeah, but—"

"Nope."

"But—"

"Don't even start," Cross warned.

His too-smart-for-his-own-good son glowered. Laughter from the other men at the table colored up the kitchen once more.

The sound of heels clicking against hardwood floors quieted them all. Soon, sixteen-year-old Cece strolled into the room looking every inch the princess that was nearly a queen. Catherine followed close behind their daughter.

Cross smiled at Cece when she came to a stop at his chair—the head of the table in his own home, always. He expected his girl to be done up in a dress with full hair and makeup as she usually did.

Instead, she was just as beautiful in skinny jeans, a blouse, with her hair in loose waves, and just a little bit of red to color her lips.

"Well?" Cece asked.

Cross reached for his daughter, and pulled her in close enough to kiss her forehead. "You look beautiful. Have a good time."

Cece beamed. "Thanks, Daddy."

A horn honked outside the Newport home.

"Go," Cross said. "I think you—" *And me*, he added silently. "—have probably made him wait long enough."

"Okay."

Cece gave him a kiss to his cheek, and then headed toward the kitchen entryway where her mother was still waiting. She just made it to there when Cross called over his shoulder, "And do make sure Juan hasn't forgotten my little chat with him."

His daughter sighed. "Yes, Daddy."

Cece was not out of the house more than two seconds before Naz huffed, and stood from his chair. Naz, too, left the kitchen without a word.

Catherine took her son's spot at the table. "He's really not happy with this whole Cece going *out* on dates, is he?"

"Well, at least he managed not to say something to Cece," Calisto said.

Cross glanced at his father. "Wait for it."

"What?"

He knew his son well.

Too well.

Once, Cross had *been* Naz ... in a way.

Cross held up a single hand, and started counting down fingers silently like they were seconds.

Five.

Four.

Three.

Two.

One.

The back door slammed.

Catherine looked at Cross with a raised brow. "Did he just—"

"Wait for it," Cross repeated.

The sound of the garage door opening whispered through the wall.

Cross gave his son credit.

Naz didn't try to be quiet.

"He's not seriously stealing one of your cars, is he?" Dante asked.

Cross gave his father-in-law a smirk. "I did."

"Pretty regularly, too," Calisto added in a mutter.

"And," Cross said, "Naz can take cars apart—you think he can't drive them, too?"

"He's going to be so pissed," Catherine said.

Yep.

Cross started counting down again—this time, out loud. "Ten, nine, eight, seven, six, five, four, three, two ... one."

The front door slammed shut. The stomp of footsteps followed before Naz came into view of the kitchen entryway. Almost six feet tall, and pissed all over.

It was amusing.

In a way ...

"What did you do to the fucking cars, Dad?"

"Took the spark plugs out," Cross returned. "You might be a fucking genius, but you came from me, *principe*. You're going to have to up your game to trick me."

Naz glared. "Where are the spark plugs?"

"Right—I'm not telling you that."

His son kept glaring.

Cross just smiled. "I told you—let your sister have her date. If I have to live through this hell, then so do you."

"Cross!" Catherine admonished.

He shrugged.

Where was the lie?

25

The Husband

Catherine POV

"What are you doing?"

Catherine continued dumping clothes into the washer. "Putting a load of clothes into the wash."

Another load.

"What does it look like, Cross?"

"It looks like something we hire the maid to do, Catty."

Catherine shot her husband a look. "Except we have an eighteen and fourteen year old who both like to change clothes twice a day—more sometimes for Cece. And you—"

"I don't change my clothes twice a day!"

"No, but you can't seem to find the laundry basket, either."

Cross quickly snapped his lips shut at that. He couldn't deny it was true. Staying silent was his second-best defense.

"We do have a maid that comes in twice a week to help with all of this, though," Cross pointed out. "You clean before the woman ever even gets here. What are we paying her for again?"

"She dusts well. I hate dusting. It's well worth the cost."

"We pay her to *dust*."

"She does it especially well, though."

Cross nodded. "Probably because it's literally the only thing she has to do when she comes here."

"And your point is ...?"

Her husband rolled his eyes, but smirked all the same. "Fine, babe. Whatever you say."

"Cece also dropped off two bags of clothes she wanted washed. Figured I should get them done before I head to Cali next week since you still don't know how to run this washer, and all."

"Hey—"

"I joke," Catherine interjected, smiling.

Cece was trying the whole college thing. Catherine could see the same disinterest she once showed for college reflecting back from Cece. She had to let her daughter figure it out on her own, though. That way, Cece wouldn't have any regrets about her choices in the end.

Like everything else in life.

Even if it scared Catherine to death.

"I just threw her stuff in with ours," Catherine said. "Might as well do it all at once when I have five minutes."

"You know," Cross murmured, leaning further into the doorway. "Cece spends just as much time living here as she does at her apartment. You still do all her laundry, and take her over enough cooked food when she doesn't come here to eat to feed a small army. I'm not sure she understands the concept of actually moving out on her own, Catty, because this isn't it. In case you were curious."

"She only stays here when Juan is out of town," Catherine replied. "I think she gets lonely without him, and we are her piss-poor substitute."

Cross glowered. "I am her father. I am not a piss-poor substitute for anything, or anyone."

Just the way his tone darkened made Catherine grin.

"It's a good thing for Juan that you like him," she said. "Otherwise, I might be concerned about his life."

"There are moments where you should probably still be concerned for his life, but I am told that's normal considering I am the father of a daughter." Cross grinned, entirely unashamed at his admittance. "And I remind him of that fact every chance I can, too."

Catherine didn't doubt it.

"So, I guess that means Cece is probably in classes, right?" Cross asked. "Since it's Friday and all—I know she has classes until supper or so."

"She didn't mention doing anything else but classes today, so yes, I imagine that's where she's going to be until she comes here to be fed."

"And Naz has his baseball practice today, so he won't be home for a couple of hours. *At least.*"

Catherine heard the suggestive dip in Cross's tone loud and clear. She gave him a look, and found he was grinning at her in that way of his.

A way that suggested sin.

Fun.

And *sex*.

She couldn't deny the heat that shot through her body as Cross looked her over with a slow appreciation. Two decades of marriage, and it only took a goddamn look to get her hot and bothered with him.

His gaze lingered on her bare legs—she was still in one of his T-shirts and a pair of sleep shorts. Shivers raced up her spine as he took a step into the room, and those dark eyes of his locked on her.

"Really?" she asked. "You find me sexy doing the laundry?"

Cross shrugged. "You're always sexy to me, babe. But also, the house is *empty*. When is the house ever empty anymore? If it's not the kids, or someone here for us, then it's someone here waiting for them."

He was close enough to touch her now, but he didn't.

Not yet.

"If you're trying to imply that it has put a damper on our sex life, it hasn't," she pointed out. "You still get laid just as much as you used to, and it doesn't slow us down."

"Maybe not in the bedroom, no."

Catherine cocked a brow. "Then what are you complaining about?"

He did reach out for then. He snagged her around the waist with one arm, and dragged her close. Kissing her without any warning at all, his tongue dipped into her mouth the second she parted her lips for him. He didn't stop kissing her until her lips were numb, and her breaths were coming out a little short.

God, she loved this man.

Still ...

After all these years.

She loved him with everything she had, and with everything she was.

Cross grasped tightly to Catherine's jaw and tipped her head back, so he could stare her right in the eyes. Their gazes locked, and just like that, the rest of the world ceased to exist. It was just them again—them and love.

"I would never complain about you for anything," Cross said softly.

"Ever?"

"Never."

"Better not."

Cross smirked. "But I wasn't lying, either. We never fuck anywhere but the bedroom now."

"And the shower," she pointed out.

He chuckled. "Mmm, true."

"Blame your kids."

"That's the thing, babe. The house is empty. No kids. No need for locked doors because there will be no walking in on us."

"Cross—"

She didn't get to say anything else. He picked her up from the floor like she weighed nothing more than a feather, and sat her down on the edge of the washer. His lips crashed down on hers as he tugged her shorts down her legs before dropping them to the floor. Her panties soon followed the same path—forgotten in a pile somewhere down below.

All the while, he never broke their kiss. And when he finally did break their connection, it was only to tip her head back, and kiss a hot path down the column of her throat. He left burning kisses across her racing pulse point, too.

Cross stepped in between Catherine's widened legs. Already, she could feel the hard ridge of his erection pressing against her center. A shot of heat darted straight down to her pussy. She had no doubt she was already wet.

God knew she was *ready*.

Unashamed and wanton, Catherine grinded her center against Cross's erection to feel more—she always wanted more of him.

"Take my cock out."

His words were a rough murmur in her ear. It sent yet another round of shivers cascading down her spine.

"So demanding," she whispered.

Cross's dark eyes found hers. "You're really going to see demanding if you don't hurry the fuck up, babe."

Catherine grinned, and kissed her husband. All the while, her hands worked at his fly. Soon, she had shoved his pants and boxer-briefs down just enough to free his thick, hard cock to her hand. She stroked him once, and then twice.

"Fuck," Cross grunted against her throat. "Stop playing, Catty."

Her laughter lit up the room, but she was quick to get his cock where she wanted it to be the most. He took her in one smooth, deep thrust. She was wet enough for him to slide right up to the hilt without taking any time at all.

Sometimes, she loved slow.

More often than not, she wanted fast.

Christ.

He filled her so good.

Stretched her open just the way she liked.

Cross's hands landed to Catherine's thighs, and his fingertips dug in hard enough to leave bruises behind. He pushed her legs open even wider—enough to make her muscles and thighs ache in the best way.

"Hold onto something."

She did—her fingers wrapped tightly around his wrists just as he started a brutal, punishing rhythm. It was enough to shake the washing machine. Hard enough to drive her crazy in the best way possible. Her fingernails scored lines into his wrists, and his teeth cut into her bottom lip before he kissed the same spot.

"Come on, babe," Cross urged. "Come for me, so I can bend you over and get you like that, too."

It was always his mouth that did it for her. She came harder than ever, and loved every second of it, too.

Cross slowed his pace just enough to kiss her through the trembling orgasm. "Fuck you look good like—"

"Ma!"

At the sound of their son's shout, Catherine jerked away from Cross with wide eyes.

"Oh, my God," she squeaked.

"Calm down," he said.

Catherine slapped him in the chest, and hissed, "You fucking calm down!"

"Ma, where are you? I forgot my gear for baseball!"

Catherine's gaze drifted to the corner of the laundry room where—sure enough—their fourteen-year-old's baseball bag sat untouched. He always left it there for Catherine to clean whatever needed cleaned.

"Ma?"

Nazio was closer now to the laundry room. Close enough that Catherine could hear his fucking footsteps.

Panic swelled in her heart.

Fear tightened around her throat.

The door was open!

"Naz," Cross called out, "do not come another step down this hallway."

"Way to be discrete," Catherine whispered.

He ignored her.

Their son's steps faltered. "Why?"

"Just ... don't!" Catherine shrieked.

The embarrassment she felt colored her tone thickly. She couldn't have even tried to hide it.

Silence followed for several seconds before Naz let out a sound of disgust.

"Please don't tell me you're—"

"Just go back upstairs, Naz," Cross said.

"Oh, God, you *are*!"

"Naz—"

"That's fucking gross!"

Cross tipped his head back, stared blankly at the ceiling, and started to chuckle dryly. She didn't know what was so funny, but he was going to be the butt end of this joke when he realized he wasn't going to get to be the one between them who *finished*.

"I put my fucking gear in there!" Naz howled.

"Just go away, Naz," Cross muttered.

"Jesus, are you naked, or something? Well … you would have to be, I guess. Oh, God—it's in my head. It's in my *head*!"

Naz's voice lessened as his footsteps echoed further away. His ranting continued on, though.

Cross gave Catherine a look and asked, "I am never going to get sex outside the bedroom again, am I?"

"Not until that kid is out of this house."

"Figured. Well, fuck. I tried."

26

The Run

Naz POV

"Naz, do you have a minute?"

Seventeen-year-old Naz glanced up from the pieces of his laptop he had scattered across the metal table. He regularly put the computer through so much abuse that he liked to take it apart, clean what he could, and replace what he needed to.

"What's up?"

His father leaned further inside the garage's doorway, and looked over the mess on the table. "Is that … what is that?"

"Pieces of my laptop," Naz said.

Cross nodded, but still looked entirely unsurprised at the admission. "You should run that cleanup program on your mother's computer—make sure there's no backdoors or open windows somewhere again."

Naz got what his father said … or rather, what he didn't say. Pretty regularly, Naz ran a program he created on his family's computers to make sure the securities and encryptions for their illegal businesses were not in any way compromised. It also made sure to keep their backdoors or unseen windows of opportunities on the computers—so to speak—firmly closed when business was done on the dark web.

One could not be too safe.

Not in their business.

"I was going to run it later," Naz said.

Cross nodded. "Good."

"So, what's up?"

His father brought out a folder from behind his back, and grinned. He waved the folder in the air like it was some kind of prize.

Naz stood up straighter instead of leaning against the table like he had been. "What's in that, now?"

"Something you have been asking about for a while."

"Oh?"

"Yeah, *principe*."

Naz lifted a brow, and then reached out to snatch the folder from his father. Cross quickly pulled the folder out of Naz's reach with a chuckle. He didn't even blink a lash at the sight of Naz's glare.

"Patience, son."

Naz scoffed. "Donati men have no patience."

Cross tipped his head to the side. "True, so here."

Naz took the folder when his father passed it over. Quickly, he opened the folder to scan the contents. All the while, his father kept grinning like he was the cat who had caught the goddamn canary or something.

It didn't even matter how smug his father looked because Naz was too caught up in the information he found in the folder.

"Holy shit," Naz said.

"It's only small," Cross was quick to point out.

"Really, though?"

Naz looked up.

His father only shrugged.

"Yeah, really. Are you up for it?"

Naz didn't even have to think about it, really. He had spent years thinking about it leading up to this moment. "Fuck yes, I am up for a gun run."

His *first* run.

"Like I said," Cross told him, putting his hands up, "it's a small run, and the buyer is a regular."

Naz nodded as he scanned the details for the buyer, and the fifty firearms he specifically requested.

"He likes them flown in, huh?" Naz asked.

"Well, he likes them flown into the first spot. Beyond that, though, they have to be driven a ways. Far safer once they've been flown in first."

"Okay."

Cross pushed away from the wall to stand straight. "So, look everything over. Sketch out all the details for your plan on this run—I will then look it all over, and decide to sign off on it or not. I'll give you about a week to get that back to me."

Naz laughed. "I'll have it back to you by tomorrow night, Dad."

Cross smirked. "Yeah, I figured."

As Naz promised, he was ready by the next night to bring his run plans back to his father.

"Dad?"

"Hmm?"

Cross peered up from the laptop screen, and Naz stepped further into his father's office. His ma sat on the window bench seat with a paperback novel in her hands.

It never failed to amaze Naz how even when his parents weren't working together, they were still *together*.

Always together.

Never apart for long.

The two could be entirely silent, yet Naz could tell they enjoyed that, too. Simply being together even in their quiet moments.

He wondered if he would ever find love like that.

A love that strong.

That fulfilling.

That amazing.

"Let me guess," his father said, "you've already got the plans for the run ready for me?"

Naz grinned. "I told you I would."

Cross put a hand out, and gestured with his fingers. "Give me what you've got, son."

Coming further inside the office, Naz passed over the folder detailing the plans for the gun run. He didn't feel particularly nervous as his father silently scanned through the details.

Naz wouldn't be offended either should his father find something wrong—unlikely—or a plan that needed changing for whatever reason. That one was far more likely only because Cross might find something that he thought could work better, or safer, in another way.

This—being a damn good gunrunner—was what his father did.

Cross Donati *was* the best of the best.

"Well?" Naz asked.

His father finished his perusal, and closed the folder.

"What do you think?" Naz asked.

Cross smiled. "It all looks good. I would be willing to go ahead with this as soon as I can get the guns moved."

"Yeah?"

"There was just one little issue," Cross added.

"What's that?"

"You planned for a partner, but didn't discuss who that would be with me ahead of time. I can set you up with—"

"Well, that's because I thought it would be you."

"Oh," Cross said.

A look passed between Naz's mother and father. An unspoken conversation Naz couldn't begin to understand. They did that far too often, honestly. Sometimes, his parents could have entire conversations in silence, and never broke a stride.

He added that into the pile of strange things about their relationship, and love. Like maybe being together for so long, and knowing each other so well was the reason why they were afforded this kind of privilege.

Finally, his mother nodded.

Cross looked back at Naz. "I guess you've got yourself a partner, son."

Naz took the folder back. "Who the fuck else would it be?"

27

The Son

Cross POV

It was the warm streak of sunlight painting bright colors across Cross's eyelids that woke him up first. And then shortly after, the soft beeping of his alarm going off reminded him that he had shit to do this morning.

Still, he didn't bother to open his eyes until he felt his wife's hand come over and push gently against the middle of his spine. Her sly way of getting him up before her so that he could make her—

"Go turn the coffee pot on, Cross," Catherine said, her voice thick with sleep.

She wasn't sly at all about this.

He groaned. "But I'm comfortable."

"You have one job in the mornings."

"A job *you* delegated to me," he grumbled, "and not one I willingly volunteered for. How I became the coffee maker between us every day, I don't know."

"I am the queen of the house."

"What about the fucking king?"

Cross finally looked over to find Catherine's green eyes glittering under the mound of blankets. He could still see the camber of her smile peeking out a little, too. It was enough to tell him she was joking.

Always trying to get a rise out of him.

"You make the *best* coffee," Catherine said with her glittering eyes and half-hidden smile. "And that is why you were delegated to the task every day of our marriage."

"Mmhmm."

Cross reached out, and grabbed hold of his wife. He yanked her from the fortress of her blankets, and pulled her into him. Smothering her half-hearted protests with a searing kiss woke up his semi-hard erection more than it already was.

He didn't mind making coffee ...

If he got a taste of her first.

"Good morning," she whispered against his lips.

"It's a very good morning now."

Catherine's light laughter lit up the room. The sweet, musical sound was a balm to his soul. A melody he had permanently imprinted on his mind. He could hear it when the house was silent, or even in his dreams.

Beauty was his life.

Love was his wife.

There was nothing about Catherine that he didn't know. There was nothing about her that he didn't love entirely.

Catherine was everything.

His everything.

"Looks like I stole all the blankets again," Catherine murmured.

Cross chuckled. "I kept a pretty tight hold on mine."

He had to.

Otherwise, she would just steal that blanket from him, too. It was just what she did.

Not that he minded.

Over two decades of marriage taught him not to mind the small stuff. They just didn't matter in the grander scheme.

"So ... about that coffee?" Catherine asked.

Cross laughed, and smacked his wife's ass over her boy shorts. "You're so goddamn spoiled, babe."

Catherine rolled off him, and preened all the while. "But who made me this way?"

He rolled his eyes at her as he moved out of the bed. "You say that like it was me. We both know you already came to me being spoiled rotten to your fucking core."

"But you love it."

Cross tugged on sleep pants, and called over his shoulder as he left the bedroom, "Yeah, can't deny that."

Her laughter chased him from the room. He really didn't mind getting up to get coffee, or to spoil her more than she already was.

Whatever made her happy.

He would do it.

Cross was in the kitchen and waiting for the percolator to finish filling the carafe when a noise from outside the entryway caught his attention. A curse, it sounded like. And it didn't belong to a voice he recognized, either.

Now, when someone unknown was in Cross's house—they signed their fucking death warrant being there.

Simple as that.

Cross reached for the gun hidden in the drawer where Catherine kept dish cloths. He had the weapon tight to his palm, and ready to fire just as the unknown intruder came into view at the entryway.

Instantly, he relaxed.

Set the gun down to his side, too.

"Who the fuck are you?" Cross asked.

The young woman—she was maybe eighteen, or nineteen—trying to sneak by the kitchen with her high heels dangling from her fingertips froze like a statue on the spot. She spun around to face Cross as he came closer.

Her wide blue eyes were a mess of smudged makeup, and smeared mascara. Sleep still lingered in her gaze, though, as if she hadn't been awake for very damn long. Her blonde hair looked like she hadn't run a brush through it that morning, and the wrinkled, sparkly club dress she wore showed off a hell of a lot of leg.

Embarrassment snaked up the girl's cheeks in a bright red.

Jesus Christ.

The walk of shame.

Oh, he knew that look well.

Sure, it had been years since he sent a woman home looking like that, and he couldn't remember a time when *he* had been the one to go home in that state. But Cross wasn't so old or foolish that he didn't recognize what he was seeing.

The young woman gaped like a fish—she was a pretty enough thing, but he doubted this was the kind of morning the woman had planned.

Cross chose to throw her a bone.

This was humiliating enough.

He waved the gun and gestured at her. "I don't want to know your name—just go. Don't even tell me a thing."

"Okay," the girl squeaked.

She was gone a second later.

Cross waited until the front door of their Newport home closed shut before he went in search of the only possible explanation for the strange young female in his house. He soon found eighteen-year-old Nazio in his bedroom doing chin-ups on the bar that hung in the doorway of Naz's connecting bathroom.

On the TV, news played.

The stereo—heavy metal.

On the white board above the head of Naz's bed—well, to Cross it looked like a bunch of jumbled, nonsensical numbers and symbols, but he knew just by seeing them enough times from Naz that it was a physics theory of some sort.

And no, not high school level shit.

Genius level physics.

All of this shit played on in Naz's room as he finished his chin-up set. The eighteen year old dropped to the floor without barely making a sound—six foot six, and two-hundred and thirty pounds of solid muscle.

Yeah, where Naz had once seemed like all long arms and legs was now a *very* filled out young man. A good two hours of every day for Naz was dedicated to fitness whether it be weight training, or hard cardio. Not because he was vain about his body, but because his body needed to be able to keep up with *him*.

He still liked his beanie, though.

That reminded Cross of when his boy was young, and still little. Before all this genius stuff had come along to make Naz a little chaotic in his life.

"Hey," Naz said as he grabbed the black marker from his nightstand. "The weather is going to be good for that gun run to Kenya."

That was what was playing on the TV.

Naz scribbled more shit Cross couldn't even begin to attempt to understand on the whiteboard, and stepped back as the TV and radio blared on in the background. The young man surveyed his formula like he was satisfied—sort of.

Cross was overwhelmed just standing there. It was too many things happening all at once, and too much noise to get his thoughts in order. Far too much movement, and everything else, too.

He couldn't keep up.

This was Naz, though.

This was Naz's everyday life.

His *mind*.

Chaotic.

Intense.

So full.

Non-stop.

"Naz," Cross said, "give me five."

Naz clapped once, and the TV shut off, Then, he snapped his fingers, and the music quieted to a dull roar in the background—much better than before.

"You want more lights on for this, or ...?" his son asked.

"Whatever, son."

Naz clapped twice, and the lights brightened. A whole set up Naz had hooked up himself. Like everything else in this damn bedroom.

Cross did not understand how he had ended up with a child that was a literal genius.

But here Naz was.

Graduated high school at fifteen. He was going into his third year of college, and would likely graduate with a doctorate within three or so years. That was, *if* Naz stayed in school and continued to work as hard as he did for his studies.

Who knew if he would?

Naz was brilliant, sure.

But fickle, too.

And restless.

Sinful.

Criminal.

Amazing, really.

The young man could attend six hours of classes five days a week, plus two hours of online studies. Then, in the evenings, he mentored under one of Cross's Capos—and Zeke, too. Naz had been doing that since he was twelve because he wanted to be a made man like nothing else.

And on the weekends?

Naz ran guns.

Sometimes with Cross, if it was a short run, but more often than not, with his partner.

"Who was that woman?" Cross asked.

Naz scribbled more nonsensical things to the white board. "Tess, or Treena ... Tyler, maybe. Something with a T, anyway."

"Nazio."

"Met her at the club last night."

"What are you gonna do if they catch your ass in one of those clubs with a fake ID, Naz?"

Nazio passed his father a look. "Buy a new one?"

Jesus.

"Naz!"

"What?"

"Since when do you break my rules—no women in this house when your mother and I are home. You know the rules."

Naz shot his father an apologetic look. "I wasn't thinking."

"Since when do you *not* think?"

Shrugging, Naz shoved his hands into the pockets of his training shorts. "When I'm buried in pussy, I guess."

Christ.

"Naz," Cross murmured, raising a brow high.

"What? It's the only time I don't have to be …"

"What, son?"

Naz gestured at the white board, and then pointed to his temple. "This."

Cross frowned.

Naz was a decent young man despite his bloodline and namesake. Sure, he was a criminal, too. Dark in his soul at times.

But he was also eighteen.

And pretty normal, all things considered.

Even being amazing like he was.

"Naz."

"Hmm?" his son asked.

"No women in the house when we're here."

"All right, Dad. Got it."

Cross smiled. "Unless, of course, it's a woman you would like to introduce your mother and I to. That, son, is a whole different story."

A chuckle answered him back before Naz said, "I don't think I am ever going to find someone to keep all of this interested for longer than it takes me to bust a nut."

"Never say never, Naz. And you know—you earn that kind of woman by being the man you think a woman like that deserves. She is never just going to be given to you."

Naz nodded, and for a second, their gazes locked. "Yeah, Dad, I know."

28

The Business

Cece POV

Cece kept her clutch close to her body as she weaved in and out of the people—very famous faces with very deep pockets, and far too many secrets to name. Working in this business of dealing drugs to the rich, famous, and spoiled since she was eighteen had taught her one very important thing: everybody had secrets to hide.

It just so happened to be that Cece, and the drugs she supplied, was a secret far too many in the elite circles kept.

Still, even though she knew a lot of the faces at the New York afterparty, she didn't feel very comfortable letting her guard down. She was twenty-two, not fourteen. She wasn't some naive girl with the belief that she held all the power.

Her mother taught her that lesson.

Not to trust anyone.

Not to give an inch to *any-fucking-one*.

A woman gave an inch, and a man took a mile. Men were goddamn predictable like that. Creatures of habits when it came to getting what they wanted. Or better yet, being denied what they wanted, and their subsequent reaction that came from it.

Cece couldn't count the amount of times she had been propositioned by the men she dealt to—or someone in their inner circles—for more than just drugs. They rarely even made a secret about asking, instead seeming to get some strange, sick enjoyment out of asking her where everyone else could hear, too.

She had no problem saying no.

She *always* said no.

They knew better, anyway.

Her body—sex—was not on the table when she showed up to answer one of their calls. She was there to hand off the drugs they wanted, and get the hell out shortly after.

Be their beautiful ghost, her mother liked to say. It was supposed to be a nothing more, nothing less kind of thing.

Some of them didn't want a ghost, though. Some of them wanted something much more tangible from Cece.

This client in particular was one ...

"Cece!"

She plastered on her fakest smile, but it still passed Mack Gordan's shit-o-meter, it seemed. The famous football player was built like a brick shithouse, and had a booming voice to match. As far as Cece knew, he'd retired a couple of years ago from the game after a bad knee injury left him practically useless.

He liked to party, though.

His reputation preceded him. Everything people said about him was true, and then some. The guy was overbearing, a little too touchy-feely, and he didn't seem to get the hint that Cece was not on his market.

Or frankly, any fucking man's market.

He was a client, though. And so, Cece sucked up her issues and uncomfortable feelings whenever she got another call that he wanted something delivered, and did her damn job. She didn't want to tell her mother that she *couldn't* handle this guy.

After all, Mack had never actually crossed a line. Not one that Cece hadn't been able to handle, anyway.

With his friends all around, a large party happening, and witnesses ... she doubted he was very threatening to her. Harmless, really.

"Hey, Mack," Cece said.

She took his hug, but didn't offer more than an awkward pat on the football player's shoulder in return. If he noticed, he didn't say anything.

Then again, he was a little too occupied by dragging his hand lower on the back of her black body-con dress until his palm rested right on the swell of her ass.

Nope.

Cece took a wide step back, and had to practically take Mack's hands off her body.

In the background, she could feel eyes blazing on her. Cece had a job to do, so she focused on that instead of looking for the man she knew was there to watch her back. He would do his job, and only step in, if he really needed to.

But she still wondered ...

"Don't you want to party with us tonight, Cece?" Mack asked.

His smile was too wide.

His pupils pin-small.

The guy was already high. Already entirely *fucked up*. And clearly not on her drugs because she had just arrived.

Why was she even here?

"Actually—"

Mack didn't let Cece finish her statement. He grabbed her wrist in his beefy palm before she could even finish, and dragged her to a leather sofa. She had all she could do not to trip in her heels, not to mention, keep herself somewhat modest when she was dragged onto the couch.

On Mack's lap.

Nope.

Nope, nope, nope.

Fuck *no*.

She was going to try to get out of this situation with as much dignity and respect she could muster to Mack, but that was all she could offer the man. At this point, he had already taken things way too far.

She didn't know if it was because he was putting on a show for someone, of if it was because he was already high.

He knew the rules.

He kept trying to cross them.

"Sorry, Mack, not to—"

Mack's hands tightened on Cece's waist to an almost painful point when she tried to stand up. "No, you can stay right where you are. Say *hello*."

Cece's gaze drifted over the people at the party. Famous faces—other football players, and socialites. In essence, people who would be more than willing to turn their cheek to something that happened because they didn't want their faces or names attached to that kind of problem. Not to mention, their precious fucking reputations.

Screw this.

Cece tried to be nice.

She tried to do this cleanly.

But she was done.

Done with Mack.

Done with being the girl who handled his calls and product.

Done with dodging his advances.

Done with his games.

Cece's hand slipped up her thigh, and while Mack's head and attention was turned on someone else, she pulled the knife out from its sheath. For some clients, Cece never even felt the need to keep protection on herself.

They were genuinely decent people—minus the occasional drug use. They never made her feel unsafe, never crowded her personal space, and never *ever* got handsy with her. Nothing like Mack had done time and time *again*.

It was sickening, really.

Flicking the knife up and around in her palm with a quick spin of the hilt around her fingertips—a cute little trick her mother taught her when she was fifteen—she had the blade resting against the side of Mack's throat that his guests couldn't see. The side that was facing the window, not the people.

Mack stiffened.

His grip on her tightened.

Cece pushed the blade harder against his pulse in his throat. "You will bleed out before an ambulance ever gets here. *Now*, you know I'm not interested. You *know* you're not supposed to touch me. Remove your hands from my body, or I will make sure the heel of my stiletto will be the last thing you see before it crushes your skull."

The whole time, she managed to keep her voice at a respectable, calm level. She didn't even let that fake smile of hers fall.

Talent, really.

It all took talent.

Cece heard Mack swallow hard a second before he let her go. A bit too hard, and with a quick shove, but she was quick on her feet. If the asshole meant to surprise her, she was already planning for a move like that.

Again ...

Men were predictable.

Cece was quick to hide her blade behind her arm as she turned to face Mack, and his now-confused looking friends. "And this is where our night—and business—ends, Mack. I will let the *regina* know to take you off her client list."

"You can't—"

"I can *do* whatever I want to do, actually," Cece said. "What, do you think the *regina* will replace me with some other poor girl for you to harass and bother? Unlikely. Have a good life. I'm sure I will see you on a new series of Celebrity Rehab in a few years."

With that, Cece turned away.

Maybe that was the mistake.

Not going in there.

Not letting Mack get too close.

No, turning her back on him.

A hand came to lock around the back of Cece's neck before she had even taken a second step away. She knew it was Mack, but her flight or fight instinct kicked in hard at the feeling of somebody *grabbing* her like that.

Nobody touched her that way.

Not without permission.

Finally, those eyes that she had felt watching her from the moment she stepped into the party made their presence known.

Juan.

The only man her mother sent to watch after her when she worked. Her only bodyguard, so to speak.

But he was so much more than that, too.

He was everything to her.

Sometimes, it was confusing. Sometimes, they were on, and they were off. Sometimes, they didn't know if they were together, or not.

It didn't matter.

Juan looked after her.

Juan was *hers*.

He was six feet, five inches of two-hundred and forty pounds of Latino muscle coming through the crowd. And the man could part a crowd just by fucking looking at it. How he managed to blend in as well as he did with that God-like face of his, and those dark eyes, she didn't know.

Cece always found him.

He could never hide from her.

Cece met Juan's gaze a second before his arm slipped around her waist. And then his fist crashed into Mack's face.

The football player had nothing on Juan.

For a second, Cece relaxed.

Juan said nothing, simply pointed at Mack bleeding on the ground like that was his one and only warning. Or maybe like he was daring the guy to stand up. If she actually cared about Mack, she would tell him the smart move was to stay on the ground and play dead like the stupid fuck he was.

He would die if he stood up.

Simple as that.

The party wasn't fun anymore.

The guests looked like frozen statues.

Someone even turned the music off.

"Come on," Cece murmured in Juan's ear. "Let's get out of here."

His arm on her waist tightened.

He'd been holding onto her since she was thirteen, and he was fifteen. Her backbone, really. He held her heart, too, and was always oh, so careful with it.

"Come on," she said again.

Juan heard her that time. "Yeah, babe, let's go."

Soon, the two were outside, and Juan was holding open the door for her to get inside his still-running Rolls-Royce. He never really failed to amaze Cece in more ways than she sometimes understood.

He wouldn't say a word about this.

Not about what happened, or how much it scared him. And she knew it *did* scare him.

He would never ask her to stop.

Never hold her back.

How could he?

How could he do that when he only ever had her back?

"Juan?" Cece whispered.

Her dark-eyed love looked back at her. "Yeah, babe?"

"I love you."

He smiled.

It'd probably been too long since she told him that. It'd been a couple months since they were official on being together again.

What even were they right now?

She didn't know.

"You know I love you, C."

Yeah, she did.

"Juan?"

"Hmm?"

"I want to marry you."

His dark eyes widened a bit, and he lifted one brow high. "Is that a proposal? Because that's not how it's supposed to work—I ask *you*."

"Yeah, well ..."

"Is it, though?"

"What?" she asked.

"A proposal."

"Have you ever thought about marrying me?"

Juan didn't even think about it. "Every day since you turned eighteen. I even asked your dad just so I wouldn't have to do it later."

"Really?"

He nodded.

Huh.

"So ... why haven't you asked?" Cece asked.

Juan pointed to the necklace Cece was wearing. It was a metal pendant of a tribal-style heart that he had given to her for her eighteenth birthday. On the middle of the heart was a single diamond. She never took it off.

Ever.

"What?" she asked.

"Let me see that, babe."

Cece took the long chain up over her head, and then passed it over. Juan closed the pendant in his hand, squeezed hard, and she heard it *crack*.

Crack like he *broke* it.

"Juan!"

He opened his palm.

The pendant was in two pieces.

In the middle, sat a ring.

The prettiest, most beautiful diamond ring. Her *mother's* ring.

"All this time?" she asked.

Juan nodded. "All this time, babe."

29

The One

Naz POV

"Shit, I can't believe Cece is actually getting fucking *married*," Luca muttered.

Naz shot his best friend—and Zeke's only son—a look. "Believe it."

The nineteen-year-old Naz was only one year older than Luca, and sometimes, it didn't seem like the two had much in common from the outside looking in. Yet, they had been attached at the hip from the time Luca was born.

Naz had a pretty good memory—he blamed it on the fucking genius thing. He could remember still being in diapers, and looking over a little gray crib to see a baby dressed in a blue sleeper looking back at him.

Luca, that was.

"Lost my chance with her," Luca muttered.

Naz barked a laugh. "Fucker, you never had a chance with my sister."

"Asshole."

"Can't help that you're fucking delusional."

Luca punched Naz in the back of the shoulder as they weaved in and out of the people flooding the house for the pre-wedding party. Cece wasn't getting married for another month, but the celebration was in full force.

Any reason for an Italian to cook.

Or party ...

They were all up for it.

Soon, Naz and Luca had pushed their way out onto the back porch where less people had gathered, and it wasn't as fucking suffocating. God knew he loved his family, but they could be a little too much when they all got together in the same house.

Usually, they threw big parties like this at one of the family's mansions. Where there was actual space between guests.

Cece wanted to have her party here at the Newport home. And Christ, their parents' Newport home wasn't even *small*. It was a three-level monster.

They just had a big ass family.

Like Juan, too, Cece's fiancé.

It was what it was.

"Here," Luca said.

He held out a freshly opened beer for Naz to take, and he was quick to down half of it in one go. He wasn't typically a big drinker, but New York was having some kind of terrible heat wave this summer, and his throat was dry from talking so much.

Another thing Italians loved.

Talking.

"So, what do you think?" Luca asked, leaning against the railing.

Naz shot his friend a cocked brow. "About what, man?"

"The whole Cece getting married thing."

"It's good," Naz said instantly.

Luca cocked a brow at that response. "Really, *good?*"

Naz chuckled, and tipped his beer up for another long swig. "You know, five or six years ago I might have had a different answer, but damn, that guy loves my sister. I don't have to worry about him treating her like shit ... or having to bury his body in cement somewhere."

His friend laughed hard. "But you know if you still need to do that someday ..."

"You will be the first fucker I call."

Luca's face split with a wide grin, and he held out his fist in offering. Naz answered it back with his own fist, and the two bumped.

Ride or die.

His brother from another mother.

"So, are you going to finally cut the fucking cord, and take the jump with me, or what?" Naz asked.

Luca sighed, and glared up at the sky like Naz was killing him. "You're never going to let that go, Naz."

"Well, it's a waste of time. You're going to be a made man like you're supposed to be. Just like I am, like my dad is, and like your dad is, too. That's what we're meant to be, Luca. You're just making the process longer by doing what you're doing now."

"So be it."

Naz shook his head, irritated.

"What the fuck are you doing in school, anyway? A lawyer, Luca, *really*? Come on."

"Says the man with a one-sixty IQ, Naz. Some of us aren't fucking blessed with a brain that just knows everything. Some of us had to wait to graduate at the right age, not early. Some of us didn't quit college because it was *boring*."

"I don't know everything. I didn't know everything from birth. I just happened to be really good at learning shit. And also, I didn't quit college because it was boring."

"Right," Luca drawled.

"I didn't. I quit because I had other shit to focus on, and getting my doctorate wasn't going to do anything for me in the long run when I was always going to be in the family business anyway."

"Whatever."

"A fucking lawyer, though. Jesus."

Luca rolled his eyes, and glanced away. "A *defense* lawyer, Naz. Who the hell else do you expect to save your ass when you need a good lawyer, huh?"

Naz stiffened, and hesitated on taking the next drink from his beer. "What?"

"You think I'm not going to be a made man?" Luca scoffed, saying, "I will, *eventually*."

"Mmhmm."

"I will, fucker. So it's going to take me a little longer than you, but that's okay. So I have to work a little harder for it between school, and Cosa Nostra, but that's fucking *fine*. You know why? Because there's a purpose to what I want to do—somebody's got to have our backs in ten, fifteen years. I don't mind being the fucker who does it, all right."

"You think that's what it's going to be?"

"What—you taking over for your dad?" Luca asked.

Naz shrugged. "I guess, yeah."

"Yeah, man, that's exactly how this is going to go down."

"All right."

Luca passed Naz a look. "All right? So what, you're going to get off my back about this school thing, now, or what?"

"Yeah, man. You do you."

Naz held out his bottle, and Luca clinked his own against the cold glass.

THE COMPANION

The two were quiet as they looked over the dark backyard. The noise level inside the house, and from the chatting people on the back deck were still quite loud. Naz didn't mind like this. He was content—at peace.

Something his brain rarely found.

It was always chaos.

Always erratic.

"Hey, Luca, Dad is looking for you!"

Naz turned at the female voice calling for his best friend, and felt a million things hit him all at once at the sight of a dark-haired, ice-blue-eyed, tall beauty leaning out the backdoor. He knew who she was.

But he hadn't seen her since she was fourteen. She was a pianist, or something. Apparently, the girl was a prodigy. Kind of like him, but without the genius aspect. They put her in front of a piano at two, and there was no taking her away from it.

Or, that's how the story went.

She was in private schools, and privileged establishments meant to cater to her unique talent, and to grow her abilities. She usually came home in the summer, as far as Naz knew, and during the holidays, sometimes.

But a lot of the time, Naz was gone. Busy with work, or running guns. He didn't stay in one place for too long, and he didn't like crowds.

Maybe he saw her in passing, but his attention had been elsewhere.

Jesus Christ.

His attention was all on her right now.

All on her.

Back then, Rosalynn Puzza—Luca's now seventeen-year-old sister—had been just a girl. Too young to catch his eye, and too quiet to be fucking noticed. She had been stuck in that awkward stage of teenage life between just coming into her own, and still being stuck as a little girl.

She was not fourteen now.

She was very much a young woman now.

Naz blinked.

His mouth went dry.

Christ.

Gone was the gangly long-armed and -legged girl with a quiet, mouse-like demeanor. She took after her mother in her features—soft, pretty lines with high cheekbones, and wide eyes. Her pink lips were painted with a gloss that accentuated the way her mouth fell into a natural pout. She had to be five foot, ten inches without her heels on—she was wearing flats with the soft pink summer dress that fell loosely over her body.

"Yeah, Rosalynn, I'll be right in," Luca said.

Naz kept staring.

She stared right back.

Luca didn't miss it, either. "Shit—why, Naz?"

He didn't say anything.

Rosalynn smiled.

Oh, damn.

The girl was a special kind of beautiful when she smiled.

"Naz, right?" she asked.

Like she didn't know his name.

Like she didn't know who he was.

She *knew*.

He liked that she teased him that way, though.

Suddenly, his brain went quiet. All that chaotic shit that just never left him alone—all the things he learned and knew that constantly kept him awake unless he worked his body to the bone was silent.

He was not Naz, the genius. He wasn't Naz, the guy working to become a made man, and the gunrunner on the weekends.

His brain was struggling to remember how to talk to a fucking *girl*. His heart actually raced, and he was pretty sure his palms were sweaty.

It was crazy.

And amazing.

"Uh ... Naz?" Luca asked, touching his beer bottle to the side of Naz's head. "You okay?"

Naz pushed his friend's hand away.

Rosalynn grinned wider. "It is, though, right? Naz?"

Finally, his incredibly *smart* brain decided to work.

Naz nodded. "Yeah, it's Naz."

"So hey," Rosalynn said, biting on her bottom lip, "maybe they're starting to dance a bit, if you want to come in and join me, *Naz*."

He didn't even have to think about it, or how he wanted to respond.

He *knew*.

Knew he finally found her.

Knew by the way his heart felt, and his soul was suddenly *alive*. Like there was some piece of him that had been waiting to find her, and now it finally had. And it was trying to crawl out of him, slipping around under his surface, and reaching out to her.

He *knew*.

His father used to say that's sometimes how it happened for men like them. All at once, and a lightning bolt that came out of fucking nowhere to strike them hard, and put them on their goddamn knees.

To remind them faith was real.

God was *good*.

Love was true.

"A dance?" she asked again.

"Yeah," Naz said. "I would love a dance with you, sweetheart."

And he knew—somehow he knew—there would come a time when

this was their party. Their families. Their day. Their upcoming wedding.
   She was the one.
   She was his *one*.
   Life and love was funny like that. Naz wasn't even going to complain.
   How could he when she was still staring at him, waiting?

30

The Wedding

Cross POV

"Smile," his mother murmured as she checked his suit.

Cross had all he could do not to roll his damn eyes when Emma fussed at his tie. A grown man, with adult children of his own, even, and his mother *still* acted like he was her baby. "The tie is fine, Ma."

"Says you." Emma patted his cheek with a warm palm, and drew his gaze to hers. There, he found childhood memories, comfort, and a mother's love. She had always been a safe place for him, of sorts. A soft spot to fall. "Now, smile."

"I am."

Emma lifted a brow. "Not *really*."

Cross tilted his head a bit to look at the mirror behind his mother. She was right. There wasn't exactly a scowl on his face, but his smile wasn't quite in place, either. "Huh."

"Big day."

"It is," he agreed.

"It's okay to be a little sad about it, too."

Cross frowned. "I don't think I'm *sad*, Ma."

"Sad about what?" Calisto barreled into the private suite with two garment bags thrown over his arm. Likely his mother's dress, and his father's tux. "What did I miss, now?"

"Cross is sad."

Emma tossed Calisto a smile over her shoulder, and his father returned it before his gaze cut to Cross.

"Sad, huh?"

"I'm not sad," Cross denied. "I'm just ..."

Calisto tossed the garment bags to a nearby chair, and came to stand beside his wife. "Not ready."

Cross looked at his father.

Calisto stared back.

For a long while, the two men stayed like that. Suspended in a silence that only the fathers of daughters could truly understand at the end of the day. He wondered if this—this heaviness in his chest, and the waiting of this day—was what his father had felt like when he gave Camilla away on her wedding day.

"That's a good way to put it," Cross settled on saying.

Calisto nodded. "I know. You're never going to be ready, son. No father ever is."

Cross let out a hard sigh, and glanced down at his hands. He fumbled with the cufflinks on his suit jacket because it was just easier than talking for the moment. He really didn't have much to say.

"Emma, go grab Catherine," Calisto murmured.

"Sure, Cal."

Cross glanced up in time to catch his mother give his father a kiss on his cheek before she quickly headed for the door.

"But be quick, Emmy, we have to get dressed," Calisto called over his shoulder.

"You always have to rush."

Calisto rolled his eyes. "That woman, I swear ..."

Cross smiled at his father's false complaints. Really, his dad loved his mom to the ends of the earth and back. It was a special, crazy kind of love that no one on the outside looking in could truly understand.

He was pretty sure even *he* didn't understand it, all things considered. Then again, he was sure people looked at him and Catherine in the same way. Like their love was something strange and strong and unobtainable.

He thanked his mother and father for that. For seeing what good, healthy, true love really was as he grew up. They had taught him how to love someone, and how to do it properly.

A good man earns a good woman.

"Juan is a good man," Cross said.

Calisto passed Cross a look. "I think so, yes."

"And I know he loves Cece like nothing else."

"Seems so."

"So why can't I—"

"You'll smile," Calisto told him. "You will smile when you need to, and when she looks at you to make sure that everything is okay today. You will smile when you have to because it's what father's do when our hearts are breaking, but theirs is so full. You will smile because you *want* to—when the time is right, and when you're feeling up to it. You *will* smile, Cross, and it will be okay."

It was like his father had taken the air right out of his lungs with that statement. Cross didn't even know how to respond.

Instead, he settled on a quiet, dumb, "Oh."

"I know—it doesn't feel like it right now."

"I'm *not* sad," Cross murmured.

And he wasn't.

He was a lot of things.

Sad was not one of them.

"It's not about being sad. It's about change, and moving into a new chapter. It's about letting go of a hand that's been holding onto yours for twenty-three years. And it's fucking fine to not know how you want to feel about that, son."

"Is this how you felt, too?"

Calisto cocked a brow. "What, when Cam married?"

"Yes."

"Of course."

"I wondered," Cross admitted.

"And for you, too."

Cross glanced up again at that statement. "What?"

"I felt like this when you married, too. Of course, I had a much longer time to prepare for you leaving than I did with Cam. You started walking ahead of me as soon as you learned how to run your mouth, and talk back. I figured by the time you were a grown man, it would be ... well, not fine, but a happy moment for me to see you marry and start a life for yourself."

"And it wasn't?"

"It was," Calisto returned, shrugging, "but it was also heavy. I didn't realize that there was still a piece of me holding onto the part of you that was still a little boy. The little boy who followed me around nonstop, and thought I was his hero. And the little boy who fell asleep in the back of my car, and played with his trains and trucks under my desk. So yes, I was happy, and it was also heavy."

Cross blinked. "But you didn't seem ... you smiled all day."

"And you will smile today, too. All day."

Catherine poked her head in the private room, and looked Cross's way instantly. "Someone said I was needed in here?"

At the sight of his wife, Cross couldn't help himself.

He smiled.

She was excited—she had been planning and planning and planning some more for this day. Cece's number one supporter, all the way, no matter what their daughter wanted to do with her life. Catherine was always there to tell their girl, *yes, be amazing.*

She was the *best* mother.

"What's up?" Catherine asked.

"I can't fix my tie right," he lied.

Catherine clicked her tongue, but didn't even question him. "All right, then."

"Cece?"

Cross held his breath just as Cece turned around to find him in the doorway of her private suite. All of the women that had been fussing over her stopped for a moment, and became still statues. He was grateful for their silence. It gave him a moment to just … appreciate how beautiful and grown up his girl was.

Her ivory lace, ball gown style wedding dress made her look like every inch the princess she had grown up as, and like the queen she would soon become. Seems she had gone with sweeping her hair up, instead of wearing it down. Her makeup was striking with dark red lips, and a smoky flair around her eyes.

He expected nothing less.

"Look at you," Cross said.

A wide grin spread across his face as he held his arms out, and came closer to his daughter. She beamed right back, already coming for him, too.

Cross caught Cece in his embrace, and brought her close enough to cup her cheeks, and make her look up at him. She smiled widely—all happy, and ready to start her life. Despite the heaviness in his gut, he smiled back.

He had to.

How could he not?

"Out, out," he heard someone say.

Cross barely got the chance to look up, and the women were leaving the room. Giving them some privacy, it seemed.

Again, he was grateful.

Now, his attention was on just one.

Cece.

She pointed at him. "Don't you make me cry, okay? Ma made me cry earlier, and they had to redo all of this makeup. My skin can't take a third round, Daddy."

Cross laughed. "You know, I don't think Juan would give a shit how you looked when you walked down the aisle, as long as you did actually walk down to meet him."

Cece fake glared. "Still!"

Quickly, Cross brought her in close, and dropped a kiss right to the middle of her forehead. For a long while, the two of them simply stood like that.

Him kissing her forehead.

Her, holding tight to his arms.

There was a time when this woman—this girl he helped create—wouldn't let him go at all. A time when her fingers had been small enough to wrap around his thumb, and he could hide her away in his arms.

He remembered a treehouse she *loved.*

A princess bed.

Books every night.

A little brother who was her very best friend.

Cross had so many things he wanted to tell her. So many things he could tell her that were running through his mind about her life, and how she had changed his with one single breath. And yet, he couldn't bring himself to say them.

Not right now.

Not yet.

"I love you, Daddy," Cece said quietly.

He nodded, and for a second, his smile faltered. She couldn't see it, though, because he was still kissing her forehead.

"I love you, my Cece."

Cece pulled back with another wide smile. "Are you ready to walk me down the aisle?"

He smiled back.

No, he thought.

"Whatever you need," he said instead.

It was just them left behind the church doors, now.
Cross and Cece.
The flower girl had gone.
The ring bearer, too.
All the bridesmaids, and Cece's maid of honor.
It was just them, now.
Her fingers tightened around Cross's arm as she glanced down at the bouquet of white and pink roses decorated with jewels.
"Did you see Nazio with Rosalynn today?" Cece asked.
She said it in a whisper, like someone might be around to hear them, and she didn't want her secrets overheard. All conspiratorial and amused like her mother was whenever Catherine had some cute secret to share.
It almost made Cross laugh, really.
"I did see them," Cross mused. "Quite a pair."
"It's only been a month," Cece pointed out.
"And yet, you can't separate them."
Zeke was both amused and frustrated that his almost eighteen-year-old daughter had suddenly found she would much rather chase Cross's son to the ends of the earth and back instead of her dreams of becoming a world-class pianist.
Thing was ... Cross knew Rosalynn would get back to her dreams, only now, with someone good and honorable to make sure she followed through. Once the newness of a first love was settled with them both, the girl would find her way back to the dreams that followed her from the time she was a young lady. Nazio would be her greatest supporter at the end of every day, and at the beginning of each morning.
Because that's who Naz was.
That's how they raised him to be.
Right now, though, Naz and Rosalynn were still trying to figure this *love* thing out.
It amused Cross to no end.
"They caught them in the confessional," Cece whispered.
Cross pressed his lips together hard to keep from laughing. It didn't help because his shoulders shook from the force, anyway.
"If that was me, you would not be laughing," Cece pointed out.

"I probably would," Cross said. "Listen, you two are my kids. I'm not going to act surprised when you all do things that I would have done. Because yes, I would have absolutely done that, Cece."

She just shook her head.

"Are you sad?" he heard her ask.

Cross laughed softly. "No."

It was a battle he had been dealing with all day. A fight that just wouldn't seem to drop. One moment, he was caught up in everything happening, and the happiness of his family. And then the next, he was thrust into a catacomb of nostalgia.

"No?" Cece asked.

"I thought I might be," Cross admitted, bringing her a little closer to his side to hug her with one arm, "but really, I'm just happy to see you where you want to be, Cece."

She beamed up at him.

Forever his little *principessa*.

A Donati queen with Marcello blood.

And a new last name on the way.

She came from the best of the best. Their legacies were ingrained in his daughter, and she would carry it well. He bet she was going to do more with it than they ever had. And he couldn't wait to watch her do it, too.

Like his son.

Because these kids ... these little people they raised to be adults were the most amazing humans on the earth. They were a perfect mix of their mother and father, but with just enough of their own quirks and personalities to make them stand out.

They were amazing.

They were going to do amazing things.

And maybe ...

Maybe that's when Cross finally felt a little more settled. Maybe that's when the heaviness left him because he knew ... this was what fathers did.

This was life.

The doors finally opened.

And Cross walked his daughter to her future.

He was still smiling, too.

31

The End

Cross/Catherine POV

Catherine

"Finally, he picks up the fucking phone," Miguel muttered, turning his back to Catherine as they headed across the tarmac. "Juan, just because you're on your honey—"

Miguel's words abruptly cut off, and then his shoulders stiffened. He pulled the phone away from his ear, and glared at the screen.

"He hung up on me!"

"Because they're on their honeymoon," Catherine reminded her friend.

"Yeah, but—"

"I would have hung up on my parents, too, Miggy."

"Don't call me that."

Catherine pressed her lips together to keep from smiling. All these years, and it was still only Cece who would get away with calling Miguel that nickname. It was still the cutest thing ever, too.

No one could tell Miguel that, though. His poor little pride might take a hit, but behind his back, he was Miggy to everybody, regardless of what he thought or wanted. It just was what it fucking was.

Catherine smacked her friend in the back of his head as she passed him by, and just as quickly, slipped into the backseat of the waiting Rolls-Royce. A ride meant for a queen. Soon—someday—she was going to give her crown up.

Hand it over.

Pass the legacy on.

She wasn't ready, yet.

Neither was Cece.

It would still happen.

Soon.

"You think you're such a smartass," Miguel said, leaning into the car.

Catherine grinned. "I know I am."

Besides, she had to keep Miguel on his toes. Cece was no longer a little girl keeping Catherine's right-hand man constantly on watch at every second of the day. Catherine liked to try and fill in to keep Miguel entertained instead.

Good friends were hard to find.

"Yeah, yeah." Miguel moved to close the door as he said, "Where to first, *regina?*"

"Business first."

She was in Cali.

Business always came first in Cali.

"Business it is," Miguel said.

Catherine looked over the information on the tablet in her hands. Nothing unusual stood out to her, or made her take pause. Nothing as cause for concern, anyway. Glancing up at the woman sitting across from her in the Four Seasons room, Catherine nodded.

"I think you are all set, Jamee," Catherine said

"Yeah?"

"I don't see why not."

The young woman beamed—happy and proud at the same time. "So, when do I start?"

"Soon," Catherine said, "but you're going to learn before you ever get sent out on your own with a list of clients. I'm glad Cece found you, though. She has a good eye for girls that do well in this business."

One of many things her daughter did well.

"Thank you, Cath—"

Catherine smiled, stopping the woman from saying anything more. "*Regina*, Jamee. It is always *regina*."

Jamee nodded. "Right, sorry."

"It's okay." Catherine gestured a finger toward the door, and said, "Either Miguel, or I, will be in contact soon. You're going to need a whole new ... well, you'll see. I think I will wait for Cece to get back from her honeymoon, but you will be well taken care of until you start pulling in money of your own. Okay?"

"Sure, yeah."

Catherine waved her fingers. "Bye."

Just like that, the young woman was dismissed. Thankfully, Jamee seemed to understand her place as one of the new upcoming girls for Catherine's organization because she quickly stood from the couch, and left the hotel room without a look back.

If there was anything Catherine hated the most from a girl, it was insolence or ignorance. She blamed her mother for that. Catrina had never accepted any kind of behavior that was less than stellar from a girl—or a man, really. It kind of passed over onto Catherine because she found little to no patience for nonsense.

Tossing the tablet to the couch, Catherine leaned back, and rubbed at her temples with two fingers. Her meetings were done for the day, and now she could relax. Another couple of days, and she would be back home with her husband where she belonged.

Oh, she loved her job.

She earned this place.

She was *queen*.

There was still a part of her yearning to get to the place where it was just her and Cross again. Her and him without life getting in the way, and business keeping them apart for days or weeks at a time.

She didn't think she was asking for very much.

"*Regina?*"

Catherine peered over at the door to find Miguel popping his head inside with a grin. "What?"

"How did that go?"

"Good."

"Yeah?"

"Cece can find them, let me say," Catherine murmured.

"She does have a knack for that," Miguel agreed.

"I think I'm going to have a shower, and then call my husband. Would you mind if we went down for dinner a little later?"

Miguel cocked a brow. "You have one more meeting."

Catherine gave the man a look. "No, I—"

"Yes, you do. One of the girls. Last minute thing."

"*Miguel.*"

"I told you. Did you forget?"

Catherine heaved a sigh. "Maybe."

Who fucking knew, lately?

"Downstairs," Miguel told her, "in the dining room. You wanted to have it there since you knew it would be closer to dinner."

Miguel offered all this to Catherine like it was gospel, and he knew what he was talking about. She really didn't have any reason to distrust him, and lately, she was kind of flaky on important things piling up.

That happened when you were planning a wedding. Although, now the wedding was over, and she was hoping to return to some semblance of a normal human being. Who was to say if that would actually be the case?

Her life was nonstop.

Chaotic.

It had always been this way.

Miguel glanced at his watch. "Ten minutes, *regina*."

Catherine grumbled under her breath. "Fine."

Cross POV

Cross was already standing when his wife entered the dining room with her sharp gaze drifting over the dining patrons. He could tell just by the stiffness in her posture that she wasn't pleased. He couldn't help but smile knowing she would soon be fine again.

As soon as …

There it was—her gaze landed on him.

Cross fixed the button on his suit jacket with a grin as Catherine came closer. She shook her head; amusement clearly dancing in her eyes.

"I thought a meeting in the dining room was a little strange," she said.

Cross chuckled. "Oh?"

"I never have meetings down here."

"Yet, you trusted Miguel."

"He's never given me a reason not to," Catherine said. "And you know, it's been so busy lately for me I wouldn't be surprised if I *did* set up an appointment with a girl, and forgot about it completely. My brain is …"

"Scattered?" he supplied.

Catherine nodded. "Yeah, the wedding did a number."

"The wedding is over, babe."

"It is."

"Our kids are all out of the house."

Catherine lifted her brow. "They are."

"Adults, now."

"Wow," she murmured, "hard to believe."

"Believe it," he said.

"And here you are, too."

Cross flashed one of his signature smiles. "I had to come see my wife. *Love* my wife."

"Is that so?"

"Catherine, that will always be so."

Sometimes, endings were just the beginning of something entirely new. For them, this was a new chapter. A different place in their lives to begin marking down memories.

"What are you thinking?" he asked.

Catherine smiled. "That I love you."

"Are you going to steal my line, babe?"

"Never."

"No?"

"Nope."

Cross reached out, and grabbed his wife to pull her into his embrace. All these years, and holding Catherine close was still the best goddamn part of his day.

"I love you, babe."

"Promise?" she asked.

"Always."

Bio

Bethany-Kris is a Canadian author, lover of much, and mother to four young sons, one cat, and three dogs. A small town in Eastern Canada where she was born and raised is where she has always called home. With her boys under her feet, a snuggling cat, barking dogs, and a spouse calling over his shoulder, she is nearly always writing something ... when she can find the time.

Find Bethany-Kris at:
Her website www.bethanykris.com or on Facebook at www.facebook.com/bethanykriswrites on her blog at http://www.bethanykris.blogspot.com or on Twitter - @BethanyKris.

Sign up to Bethany-Kris's New Release Newsletter here: http://eepurl.com/bf9lzD.

Other Books

John + Siena

Loyalty
Disgrace

Cross + Catherine

Always
Revere
Unruly
The Companion

Guzzi Duet

Unraveled, Book One
Entangled, Book Two

DeLuca Duet

Waste of Worth: Part One
Worth of Waste: Part Two

Standalone Titles

Effortless
Inflict

Donati Bloodlines

Thin Lies
Thin Lines
Thin Lives
Behind the Bloodlines
The Complete Trilogy

Filthy Marcellos

Antony
Lucian
Giovanni
Dante
Legacy
The Complete Collection

Seasons of Betrayal

Where the Sun Hides
Where the Snow Falls
Where the Wind Whispers

Gun Moll Trilogy

Gun Moll
Gangster Moll

The Chicago War

Deathless & Divided
Reckless & Ruined
Scarless & Sacred
Breathless & Bloodstained
The Complete Series

The Russian Guns

The Arrangement
The Life
The Score
Demyan & Ana
Shattered
The Jersey Vignettes

Find more on Bethany-Kris's website at www.bethanykris.com.

Made in United States
Orlando, FL
06 May 2023